Eighty Dollars to Stamford

Other Works by Lucille Fletcher

Sorry, Wrong Number
Night Man
The Daughters of Jasper Clay
Blindfold
. . . And Presumed Dead
The Strange Blue Yawl
The Girl in Cabin B54
Night Watch (a play)

Eighty Dollars to Stamford

Lucille Fletcher

Random House: New York

Library of Congress Cataloging in Publication Data
Fletcher, Lucille.
Eighty dollars to Stamford.
I. Title.
PZ4.F613Ei   [PS3556.L424]   813'.5'4   75-8536
ISBN 0-394-47544-5

Manufactured in the United States of America
9 8 7 6 5 4 3 2
First Edition

Eighty Dollars to Stamford

One

It seemed a lucky break, a bonanza, the first good thing that had happened to him in three months of part-time cab-driving. Dave was twenty-eight years old, a Brooklyn schoolteacher, and a widower. The time was dusk on a spring evening, and he had just pulled out of the fleet garage.

She was standing half a block away when he spotted her under a street lamp—a slender blonde in a long black coat, waving at him, signaling for him to stop. It was a desolate street near the Hudson River and no place for any woman to be stranded after dark. He drew over to the curb at once.

"Cab?" He reached back, unlatching the door.

Yet she seemed to hesitate. On that street of shadows and gloomy warehouses she stared at him, and then, with one hand on the door handle, she was peering into the cab, first at him and then at his identification photo, as if to assure herself that he was someone it was safe to be with. In the light of the street lamp she was beautiful, with long corn-silk hair framing a face with finely chiseled cheekbones. The long coat hung loose and unbuttoned, revealing a very short skirt and long slender legs in boots.

"Okay?" He grinned into the wide blue eyes rimmed with mascara.

"Yes." Dimpling, she smiled back at him, and then climbed into the cab.

"Where to?" he asked.

Her voice was soft, refined, with a musical quality. "I'd like to go to Stamford, Connecticut, please."

"Stamford, Connecticut."

It was at least an hour's ride from Manhattan, and a plum assignment.

"Can you get me there by eight o'clock?" she asked.

"Well . . . sure."

The time was twenty minutes of seven. Dave had no idea of the rates to Stamford, but before he could say anything she was saying, "You can take the Triboro and the Bruckner Expressway—or just drive over to the West Side Highway and follow the Hudson River." She paused, and he heard the rustle of crisp bills. "I'll pay you eighty dollars, okay?"

"Eighty dollars?"

"Is that enough?" she asked. "For the round trip? Because, you see, I'd like you to bring me back. I'm only going to be up there an hour."

"An hour."

"Here." She thrust the roll of bills at him, bills bound by a rubber band. "Please take it now, driver, and let's just go. Or I'll be late."

"O–kay, miss."

He stepped on the gas pedal.

The moon was full. The sky was cloudless. Fate, he thought, was being kind to him. Eighty dollars . . .

Her destination was a house on a road called Red Mill Lane. "It's about eight miles from Stamford," she said. "Off the Merritt Parkway take the second exit and then I'll direct you the rest of the way."

"Fine," he said.

"Why don't you start off with the West Side Highway?"

It was a beautiful trip with not much traffic, and they made excellent time up the moonlit parkways. By seven-thirty they were plunging into the maze of twisting two-lane roads that service the back country of fashionable Connecticut.

The moonlight glimmered on woods and dim-lit settlements, handsome estates and quaint white houses. He could hear the distant rushing of water and occasionally glimpse the silvery vista of a lake or reservoir. Red Mill Lane was deep in the country, a long road sloping steeply upward and topped by a lighted church steeple. He could see no sign of a house.

"It's over there—on the right," she said. She was pointing to two white gateposts at the foot of the long hill. "You can let me off right there."

"Here, lady?"

He had pulled up in front of the gateposts.

"Yes, I'll walk in," she said. The house was nowhere in sight. The driveway was bordered by immense pines.

"You don't want me to drive you up to the house?" he asked.

"You can't. There's a chain—with a sign on it. See?"

There was indeed a chain across the shadowy entrance, looped between the gateposts. Hanging from it was a small sign: PRIVATE DRIVE. NO TRESPASSING. "You're sure this is the place?" Dave peered into the darkness.

"Yes. Just wait here, please." Her voice had sunk to a whisper. She slipped quickly out of the cab. "I'll only be gone an hour." She came close to his window. "And please don't tell anyone I'm here, if they ask you. Promise? It's important. Nobody is to know."

"Okay," Dave replied.

In the moonlight, on the shadowy road, she was looking at him anxiously, one hand still on the taxi door. "*Please!* Don't forget!" Then she turned and hurried toward the gateposts.

Gracefully lifting the skirts of her long coat, she stepped lightly over the chain and flitted off down the driveway in the shiny, high-heeled boots. Her pale hair melted into the shadows, her light footsteps died away.

He sat in the cab for about five minutes, then got out, closed the door quietly, and stepping over the chain, started up the driveway.

It twisted and turned beneath the tall motionless pines which formed a dark pungent canopy above his head. Underneath his feet were pine needles. Finally the trees thinned, and he stepped into an open clearing. Facing him, spectacular in the moonlight, was a huge pond, and beyond the pond a beautiful white house.

It was enormous, with steep roofs and many chimneys. Rambling and Colonial in design, it was backlit by the moon and framed by fine old trees. But no lights were visible. Every window facing him was dark.

He moved closer to this dreamlike scene. Awed by its sheer

5

beauty, he let his eyes rove over the spacious sweep of lawn, the antique architecture, the manicured shrubbery and the beautiful bright pond in which all this splendor was reflected as in a vast mirror at his feet. It was a dream estate, a rich man's Eden, but it looked unoccupied, deserted. There was not a car on the parking lot, not a floodlight illuminating the main house or any of the outbuildings.

He moved on.

He made a circuit of the house. A brick patio led to a Dutch door through which he peered, seeing only darkness. There was a greenhouse farther on, with a rake and wheelbarrow outside, a huge garage, and even a tennis court with the net up. Beyond the tennis court were woods looking out over railroad tracks. But there were no lights anywhere. No people. Not a soul.

Across all the downstairs windows curtains were drawn. Upstairs the shutters were closed.

Whatever was happening in that house was happening in the dark, and Dave finally imagined what it must be.

Half an hour had gone by.

Frowning, he returned to his cab.

If he had a spare minute from cab-driving, he would usually try to phone his mother-in-law in Brooklyn to check on his two boys. Up the road, at the top of the long hill, the church steeple was still floodlit, and halfway down the slope he could see a couple of dim lights showing through the trees. He started trudging upward in search of a phone booth, his shadow slanting on the road beside him. He strode rapidly, a tall young man with shaggy dark hair and somber brown eyes, hands thrust into the pockets of his tan windbreaker, lips pursed in a toneless whistle under his thick dark brown mustache.

A boy on a bicycle appeared over the brow of the hill and came coasting rapidly past him. After the boy had disappeared, Dave was again aware of the deep country quiet, the privileged isolation of this wealthy community which was so very different from his own. Its silence, its aloofness chilled him, and he longed to hear his mother-in-law's voice and the piping voices of his little sons. But there was no phone booth anywhere, the church was locked, and he walked slowly back, pausing halfway down the hill to gaze at a barn-red house nestled on a rocky ridge. In its dimly lit upstairs windows were white ruffled curtains which reminded him of Fran. He stood looking at them sadly, moving on only when a car approached, its headlights bathing him in a blinding glare.

"Like a lift?" The voice was pleasant, male. The car was a black Thunderbird.

"No, thanks." He stood blinking in the light, but the car did not move on immediately. He caught a glimpse of the man behind the wheel, a boyish-looking man with light hair.

"Anything the trouble?"

"No, sir," Dave replied. Finally the car moved forward, turning in just before it reached the top of the hill at the house with white curtains.

Again intense silence settled down, broken only by the sound of his feet over macadam. He looked at the radium dial of the watch Fran had given him for his twenty-fifth birthday. Ten minutes to nine.

The pine branches lifted in the mild spring wind. Their shadows wove dim patterns on the moonlit driveway. In the stillness, far off, a dog began to bark. And the sign hanging from the chain went tink-tink-tink, as the second hand went slowly ticking around.

At precisely nine o'clock he heard quick footsteps.

She appeared as she had disappeared—on the run. Her long hair swayed about her shoulders, and her long coat flowed out behind the boots. She crossed the chain. Her face was bland, the face of a bisque doll.

"Any trouble?" she whispered.

"No," Dave said.

"Well, *thank* you. Thanks for waiting." She flashed into the back of the cab. He had the door open. She inched it closed. "Now can you take me back, please? You see, it *was* just about an hour."

"Where to?"

"Oh—a subway would be fine."

"I'd be glad to drive you home," Dave said.

"No . . . the one at Fifty-seventh and Sixth is fine." Her voice became urgent. "Come on, please. Let's go."

He started the engine and they lurched away from Red Mill Lane, the chain and the two gateposts.

"And would you mind turning the heater on?" As he glanced

back, he saw that she had cast herself against the seat and lay huddled in a corner, with her golden head drooping. She was shivering.

"Are you okay, miss? Is anything wrong?"

"No. Nothing," she said in a dull voice.

She had not talked on the ride up, and she said nothing most of the way back, merely lit one cigarette after another, filling the overheated cab with smoke and the acrid odor of burning mentholated butts in the overfilled ashtrays. In the flare of a match he glimpsed her face in his rear-view mirror, and it looked sad and pensive. He heard her sigh.

"You're sure you're okay, miss?"

"Yes, thank you."

Her voice was clear and sweetly precise. It reminded him of a delicate bell, the bell of a French clock his mother had had on the mantel when he was a very small boy. As a cabdriver, Dave was very conscious of voices. Often they were all he knew of his passengers, cut off as he usually was by a wall of safety glass and grilled partitions, all devised to protect him from the strangers behind his back. But voices provided clues to character, and her voice intrigued him. He could not place it in any part of the United States. He could not place its purity of diction in any part of the world.

"Cab warm enough for you?" he asked.

"Yes, thank you."

He wanted to make her talk—partly for the pleasure of hearing her voice, and partly because his mind was seething with curiosity. Why an hour? And why the secrecy? What could she have been doing in that house for just an hour that would justify an eighty-dollar cab ride? And why the urgency, the need to be on time, if the house was pitch-dark? Dave kept toying with the possibilities.

Back there on the lawn of that huge estate, gazing up at the dark windows, he had figured her for some high-priced whore whom some rich guy had summoned to Stamford for an hour, but now he wasn't quite so sure. Maybe she actually belonged in that white house; she was a daughter or a wife or an ex-wife or some relative who had sneaked up there on some special errand she didn't want the neighbors to know about.

"You come up to Stamford often, miss?"

"No. This is the first time—ever," she replied.

"But you seem to know the way."

"I have a map right here in my purse. I was told how to get there."

She lit another cigarette, rolled the window down, and tossed out the empty pack.

"Beautiful house," Dave said.

"You mean you saw it?"

"Just walked down the driveway . . . looked around a little," he said.

"Well, I wish you hadn't." Her voice rose slightly. "*Please* never tell anyone, promise me. Not even your wife. Promise?"

"I don't have a wife," Dave said somberly.

"All right then. Just don't tell *anybody*. Not even your girl friend. Otherwise I'll be in trouble—*awful* trouble. Do you swear?"

Dave grunted. "Hell, lady." He half laughed. "I don't even know who you *are*."

"Well, just don't mention it at *all*. Don't say you even took anybody. That's a must and I really mean it." She sounded very tense. "Just erase this from your mind . . . your records."

He did not reply. Her face disappeared from his rear-view mirror. When they arrived at the subway station she again came round to his window and looked in at him anxiously with the big blue eyes.

"Please. I would bless you to the end of my days if you wouldn't tell anybody."

"Why?"

"All right then—don't!" The blue eyes flashed. "Forget about it."

She hurried away.

With blond head held high, hair swinging about her shoulders, she ran across the sidewalk and down the stairs of the Fifty-seventh Street station. She vanished from his view and his responsibility, even his conscience, forever, he thought—like all the other passengers he had ever driven—in the vast soulless city of New York.

He owed her nothing. He would never see her again.

Slowly he left the curb and headed toward Broadway.

Two

Dave did not work the following evening—or the next one or the next. It was the Passover and he spent the weekend dutifully at home with his mother-in-law and his two sons.

Momma, a short chunky woman with iron-gray hair, had been keeping house for him ever since the death of his wife, her only child. In spite of her grief, she was still a lady of fierce will and energy, and for this High Holiday she had scrubbed and waxed the four-room apartment in Flatbush, laundered the curtains, and spent long hours cooking and chopping. At sundown they all sat down to a splendid Passover meal. Momma lit the candles; Dave said the appropriate prayers. As the male head of the family he told his little boys the ancient story of Moses and the Red Sea—and the Pharaoh who'd been flouted three thousand years ago.

From atop the television set in the living room Fran's face in a silver frame kept watching, smiling gravely in the melancholy light of the candles. Dave tried not to look at her or think about her as he sat in the stuffy dinette carving chicken and passing plates to his two boys.

"Eat! Eat!" Momma was spooning food into Baby Jeremy's mouth and watching Dave with her sharp dark eyes. "What's the matter? You're not eating, Dave? You don't like the chicken? It's cold? I should warm it in the gravy?"

"No, Momma. It's delicious."

He attacked his food. He smiled at his children. Yet even as his eyes rested on their solemn little faces, at Jeremy in his highchair and Joel propped on a couple of phone books, he felt the familiar stab of agony. For in each child he saw some echo of his wife.

The eyes of thin six-year-old Joel were Fran's big gray ones—luminous and sensitive. And fat cheerful Jeremy had inherited her beautiful hair. It was the same soft chestnut and curled around his ears like hers.

"I've got to get some air." He pushed back his chair.

Riding down in the elevator, then striding along the streets of Flatbush, he breathed deep gulps of air and fought for self-control.

Fran had been dead for six months, and he had tried his best to accept it; but there were times, particularly at night in the apartment, when he felt so stifled by his grief and rage that he could not sit still. He had to bolt from the flat and walk for blocks, sometimes ending up as far afield as Sheepshead Bay or Bay Ridge without realizing how he had gotten there. In six months he had become a loner, a wanderer, and it was quite understandable to those who knew the tragedy which had befallen him.

Six months before, Dave and his young wife Fran, the mother of his two children, had been returning from a late party in Manhattan.

On a deserted corner of Fifth Avenue at two o'clock in the morning, they had been crossing with the light, laughing and swinging hands, when a car, a small black convertible, came careening around from a side street and struck Fran, sideswiping Dave, who was knocked aside by the violent impact.

Before his horrified eyes Fran was catapulted into the air, like a ninepin. He struck the pavement and passed out, but just before the moment of unconsciousness, he saw the man's face turning to look at him from the black car like a carved mask on a pivot. The man's hair was gray, his features hawklike. One eye glittered, as it fixed on Dave. The other had a black patch over it.

When Dave regained consciousness, the car and the man were gone. The street was empty, and only the body of Fran, a little bloody crumpled heap of clothes, was lying there on the sidewalk, with the dark stores staring, the yellow autumn moon, the long waxed avenue.

Dave began to howl then, like a dog, and he was howling when they found him . . . when they got him into the ambulance. He was in the hospital, Bellevue Hospital, for a week. They let him out only to attend her funeral. All he could say was "Who is he? Let me kill him. Find him. Bring the bastard to me." He would hold his hands up, clench them, then begin to shake. And even now, six months later, the very memory of the man in the black car could make his hands shake uncontrollably as though they ached to grip themselves around the throat of his wife's murderer.

Fran had been his childhood sweetheart—the only girl he had ever loved. She had been there when his father and mother died, one after the other, in the space of a year, when Dave was barely sixteen. She had helped him, encouraged him to get an education, to teach, to help the slum kids as she had tried to help them. He thought of her as a saint, an angel.

But the man was never found. No one but Dave had seen the accident. And he had been too stunned to notice more than that the car was black, small and a sports car, and that it looked foreign. Small foreign sports cars were a dime a dozen, the police said. And as for men with eye patches, they were fairly common too.

"Liars. Slobs," Dave muttered, when he was released from Bellevue and sent home to his empty flat, his little boys, his sad-faced mother-in-law. For weeks thereafter he conducted his own search, haunting filling stations, body shops, foreign car dealers, automobile clubs. He ranged far and wide—as far as New Jersey, Westchester and Long Island. He telephoned foreign embassies and talked to insurance companies—all to no avail. The man had vanished. Out of nowhere he had come and into nowhere he had returned—like a demon out of hell.

Yet Dave knew that he was real, and Dave burned to find him someday. He knew that he would recognize that livid hawklike face the minute that he saw it—if he ever saw it again. It was a face one could never forget, with its thatch of graying hair, the one cold glittering piercing eye, the other hidden under an eye patch. And when he saw it, he knew he would not hesitate to kill.

Even now, six months later, there was no doubt whatever in his mind.

But meanwhile it was Passover. He returned to the apartment. The kids were exhausted from all the rich food and soon were ready for bed. After he had tucked them in, he helped Momma with the dishes.

"So—everything okay now?" she asked. "You feeling better, Dave?"

"Yes. How about you, Momma?"

"I'm all right." She hung the dish towel up elaborately. She began scouring the roasting pan. "So what else is new with you? I didn't see you last night to talk to."

Usually she sat up for him on the nights when he drove, and fixed him tea and a sandwich, no matter how late it was when he got home. She liked to listen to his adventures, to hear about all the crazy people he encountered; sometimes, just to amuse her, for he pitied her and admired her bravery, he would exaggerate the humor or the drama of a situation. But she had been asleep on the sofa when he arrived home on Thursday, and he had tiptoed past without waking her.

"What kept you out so late?" she asked.

"Oh, I stopped off. Had a drink with a couple of the boys."

"A drink?" She bristled, then smiled and nodded. "Good. That's good, Dave. It's helping, then, the cab-driving? You're relaxing? Making friends?"

"Yes, it's therapy."

"Therapy-schmerapy. It just shouldn't make you into a bum yet."

"Momma, fat chance," he said.

"I know, I know. You're a good boy." She kept looking at him with a mixture of affection and suspicion. "Only it seems to me you had another coupla drinks, after you got home, didn't you? I found the schnapps bottle."

"I couldn't sleep," he said.

"You couldn't sleep." With arms akimbo, she studied him as she stood beside the sink. "Anything bad happen?"

"Of course not."

"Somebody robbed you? Mugged you?"

"Momma!"

She tossed her head. "It's a crazy business. Pulled a knife maybe?"

"Nothing. Everything was fine."

"Hm. Well." She turned back to the roasting pan. "I just thought there was something funny about you. You were so quiet."

"I'm always quiet."

She sighed. "All right, Dave." The conversation was becoming ridiculous. She was his mother-in-law, his best friend, and there was no reason not to tell her about the strange girl he had driven to Stamford, the blonde who had spent an hour in a pitch-dark house, paid him eighty dollars and begged him not to tell anybody. It was the kind of story she would have loved to hear—romantic, mysterious, all about rich people and their scandals and extravagances. The eighty dollars would have thrilled her. It was more than he often earned in a week of cab-driving.

But he did not tell her—that night or the next or the next. And it would have been much better if he had.

Three

The first thing he saw was her white umbrella hovering like a dome-shaped balloon under the same street lamp in that neighborhood of warehouses. It was precisely quarter of seven on the Monday following Passover, and again he had just started on an evening of driving. She was wearing the black coat and black boots, and as he came closer, peering through the rain and his moving windshield wipers, he could see the glistening tips of her blond hair curling around her shoulders and the soft blur of her face through the transparent plastic.

"Hi." He drew up beside her, rolling the window down. "Need a ride?"

"Oh, *yes.*" The umbrella bobbed back and her face emerged, dewy and radiant. "I'm so *glad* to see you. How fortunate!" She was in the cab in the next minute or so, and slamming the door shut even as he asked the question.

"It's not Stamford again, is it?"

He turned around, looking back at her.

She was collapsing the umbrella. Her head was averted from him. "I'm afraid it is," she said in a subdued tone. Then she raised her eyes to him, smiling timidly. "Isn't that awful, on such a terrible night?" She leaned forward, blinking the dark eyelashes. "But it's only for an hour again . . . and . . . here's the money." Lowering her eyes again, she stuffed the green wad of bills into the money compartment. "Eighty dollars. Just so we get there by nine." She settled back.

"Is this going to be a regular thing?"

"A regular thing? Oh, no. It was just a hurry call. I only heard about it an hour ago."

"I see."

He had not yet moved from the curb. He picked the money up—all twenties, crisp new bills, bound by a rubber band.

"What's the matter? Isn't eighty enough?" she asked.

"It's plenty," Dave said. "But I can't promise to keep it quiet again."

"You *did* keep it quiet though? Last Thursday?"

"Yes, but not tonight."

"Why not? It's absolutely necessary."

"Look, sister," Dave said. "I faked one report." He picked up the trip sheet and waved it in her direction. "I can't fake another. What do you want me to do—lose my license? It's the law—a police regulation. We're supposed to keep a record."

"All right." She sighed deeply. "But if you did it once, why can't you do it again? I'll never ask you for another favor. Please. Just this once, please? Won't you help me?" The sweet young voice trembled.

"If anybody hears about it, I'm out of a job," he said.

"Yes. But who's *going* to hear about it? *I'm* certainly not going to tell on you."

She stirred uneasily in the shadows. "Please, please. It's important—and I'm so late already." He could hear a note of desperation in her voice. "Please don't make me stand out there in the rain looking for another taxi."

In slow motion he left the curb, the streetlight and the grim façades of the old stone warehouses. Rain drummed on the cab roof and streamed down his windshield with renewed force as he headed out of the city.

It was a lousy night. Gone was the elation of the first ride in the moonlight. On the parkways this miserable evening long streams of southbound cars streamed by, like endless caterpillars of light, flashing their high beams in his face and turning the rain pouring down his windshield into a glittering curtain of diamonds and crystals. Filthy water from puddles and potholes splashed against him every time a car passed by. With all the windows closed, the cab grew steamy, the air oppressive. As they moved northward, lightning flickered and the mutter of thunder could be heard.

"What time is it?" she asked.

She had sat there smoking, saying nothing, all the way up through the storm.

"Almost nine."

"Oh, dear. How far away are we? I can't see anything."

"We're almost to the exit."

The last few miles through the dim back country roads were a maze of slippery macadam, blind curves, and spates of fog which floated up from the invisible water they were passing, shrouding bridges and signs and crossroads so that he barely crawled a good part of the way.

At twenty minutes past nine, the lighted church steeple glowed faintly in the distance. "Thank God," she breathed, and then asked tensely as he slowed the cab and stopped, "What's wrong?"

"Look." He pointed toward the rising slope of Red Mill Lane dead ahead. Stretched, nose to nose, along the dark wet roadway were cars parked almost to the top of the hill. "Somebody seems to be giving a party."

"Oh, dear. *Dear!*" She threw herself back against the seat. "What are we going to do now?"

"Turn around and go back to New York?"

"Oh, no. No. I *have* to be there—for at least an hour," she said.

"But somebody's sure to see you—with all those people around."

"I'll just have to risk it." Her voice shook. "Drive over there between the gateposts. See? There's a space between them."

"Why don't I *drive* you in, for God's sake?"

"You can't. The chain's up."

"I'll unhook it."

"No! *Please!*" Her voice rose. "*Please*—stay here outside."

In a flash she had the cab door open. She was out and running, bareheaded, toward the driveway. In the teeming rain she ran with her long black coat flapping about her ankles, then leaped the chain and careened off in the high-heeled boots as though she were pursued by demons.

Dave gazed after her sourly.

He parked the cab between a Cadillac and a red MG, thus blocking the driveway entrance. Then, turning the collar of his windbreaker up, he started walking up the driveway in the cold wet rain. From the barn-red house up the hill where the party was being given, he could hear faint music, the thumping of a drum and the twang of an electric guitar. The sound of this neighboring gaiety only emphasized the darkness and rain-swept desolation of these grounds.

Again no lights were visible, no cars, no human beings. Rain pattered on the black pond water and slashed across the tennis court. Standing under a tree, he paused, looking up at the closed shutters. By now in one of those bedrooms, she was already probably undressed. He could envision her nude white body and her long fair hair flowing over her naked shoulders. On a chair, tossed carelessly, he could see the coat, the muddy patent-leather boots.

He shrugged. He turned away. He felt disgust, and then to his surprise he felt something more—a twinge of resentment that seemed close to jealousy. This disturbed him, and trudging back up the driveway he stepped over the chain, got into his cab and turned the radio on.

A basketball game was being broadcast, and sitting there with his hair still soaking, he hoped it might be the Knicks, but it was only the University of Bridgeport playing Colby. He clicked it off. It was by now five minutes after ten.

A car door slammed.

He frowned, rubbed at the windshield with his sleeve, and peered out. Through the rain and mist people were walking toward him, down the road from the barn-red house. The party was breaking up early for one that had sounded so lively less than half an hour ago. Headlights flashed and car engines started as trooping along under umbrellas came a handful of people whose cars were parked directly in front of Dave's cab or directly behind it.

He sat erect, staring straight ahead, as two middle-aged ladies in raincoats edged by on their way to a station wagon two cars back. He tried to lounge nonchalantly as a white-haired couple under a large black umbrella came plodding along through the puddles and finally climbed into the Cadillac ahead. By twenty minutes past ten only the red MG parked behind him remained unclaimed.

The lights in the barn-red house went out.

Dave was watching the driveway intently when suddenly he

heard a cry in the distance, and running down the road came a young woman in a yellow sou'wester and slicker. Her face was invisible. She ran past him in the pouring rain and scrambled into the MG. He heard the engine starting, and at the same time, from afar, a man's thin voice.

"Muffin!"

The engine roared.

The man could now be seen running, or rather weaving unsteadily, down the road. "Muffy! Wait! Don't leave!" he called. He was very drunk, a gray-haired man in a dark blue blazer and pipestem pants. "For God's sake!" he cried in anguish as the MG shot forward. As it sped up the long steep hill she shrilled, "Go home! Get lost!" and then her taillights vanished over the hill.

"Aw!"

For a few moments the man just stood there, swaying in the rain. He reached one hand out into thin air as though trying to support himself, then, shaking his head, circled the wet roadway a couple of times. On the third orbit he spied Dave and halted. A smile lit up his face.

"Hey!" Staggering forward, he waved and called, "Take me to Westport?" He peered into Dave's window. "Lost my ride." He gestured up the hill. "Need some transportation."

"Sorry."

"Don't say no, Buster. Gotta get there, or she'll lock me out." He grabbed the door handle. Dave had locked the door. "Come on. Be a good scout." He fumbled in the pocket of his skin-tight soaked slacks. "Five dollars? Ten? Come on, chum. Who you waiting for? Party's over. Everybody's gone."

"Sorry."

"Fifteen dollars," said the drunk. "Crazy little kid. She told me to meet her at the party." He waved the bills. He glowered outside Dave's window. "Whatcha doing here anyway?" he yelled. "Nobody's in there either." He gestured toward the gateposts. "Ferguson's away. That house is empty."

Dave stared at him.

"Oh, the hell with you." The man backed off, muttering. Then he kicked a tire. "Stinking son of a bitch." Turning to leave, he shouted, "Chosen people. Up the chosen people." Then he began to run.

But Dave was staring at the driveway, the dark pines, the sign, NO TRESPASSING.

"Empty . . . Ferguson's away . . . that house is empty."

Fog floated down the hill and rain drummed on the roof of his cab. Minutes passed. They seemed like hours. And then he heard her whisper.

"Is it okay?"

She was standing like a ghost inside the gateposts underneath the pines. When he turned his head, she hurried toward him with her long coat sopping, her nose buried in her coat collar and her hand spread over the top of her blond hair.

"Let's go." She pulled the door open. "Make a U-turn. I don't want him to see me."

"He's gone long ago," Dave said.

As he started the cab, she crouched down on the floor behind him. "I'm cold. I'm frozen." As he made the turn he could hear her teeth chattering, and in his rear-view mirror he could see her huddled on her knees and swaying with the motion of the cab.

"Do you have a rag or anything I could dry my hair with?" When they reached the Merritt Parkway she crawled back up on the seat.

Dave had an old towel. He passed it back to her. "Thank you," she said in the delicate bell-like voice, and then added, "I heard what that awful man said to you. It was hateful. And I'm sorry."

Dave said nothing.

"And that stupid girl," she sighed. "It was all so unfortunate, such an absurd thing to have happen. But thank you for your loyalty—your silence."

He sat there, still saying nothing. He waited until they were a few miles down the Merritt Parkway. Then he spoke. "That drunken guy said the house was empty. Is it empty?"

She did not reply.

"He said that Ferguson was away. Who's Ferguson? The owner of the place?"

There was a long silence.

"Who's Ferguson?"

"I don't know. I have no idea," she said quickly. "But it's empty—yes. The house is empty."

"It's been empty all along?"

"Yes," she said, after a long pause.

He chuckled mirthlessly. In the rear-view mirror he could see her pale, drawn face, the chiseled bones of her cheeks lit by a match flame. "I know it's none of my business," he said. "But I don't get it. If nobody's in that house, then what the hell is going on?"

"Nothing," she replied. And then he heard the panic, the hysteria creeping into her voice. "I'm sorry, I can't possibly tell you. So please don't ask me any more questions, please. If you do, I'll only have to lie to you. And I'd hate to lie, I'd *hate* to!"

Four

Down parkways sleek and slick as oil they traveled, and he could hear her rubbing at her hair and sighing. When she spoke again her voice was soft and bell-like, with the plaintive self-pity of a child's.

"Please don't be angry at me. I hate people to be angry."

"Who's angry with you?" Dave said from the front seat. "I've got no right to be. I'm just the cabdriver. You paid me eighty dollars. It's not my business what you do with your life."

"But I want you to be my friend," she said.

Briefly he turned his head. She was patting her hair with the old towel, and it fell about her shoulders like tangled wet silk. In the black sweater and short skirt she looked like a teen-ager, like one of his students.

"I do," she said softly. "You're nice. One of the nicest people I've ever met."

He could hear the wheels of the cab humming over wet cement. The dark shrubbery and trees lining the median strip of the parkway passed like landscaping in a cemetery.

"Is it drugs?" he asked.

"*Drugs?*"

"Yes. That place isn't a drop for a drug ring, is it?"

"*What?*" She sounded genuinely flabbergasted.

"And you're not the delivery girl?"

"Of course not." She began laughing in a strange breathless way. "What a thing to think of. Do I *look* like any drug addict? Talk like any junkie?"

"They come in all varieties."

"I *hate* drugs, I despise them. I've never even tried marijuana." Her voice rose. "Drugs! Why, it never ever occurred to me you'd have such a suspicious mind."

"I'm a cabdriver," Dave replied.

"But you're not *just* a cabdriver."

The way she said it was just enough to make him turn his head and frown. "What makes you think so?"

"Why—everything!" Her tone was light and lilting. "Your voice. And your appearance." She leaned forward. "Are you an actor? Or a student, maybe?"

"I'm a teacher," Dave said flatly.

"A teacher? A *school*teacher?"

"What other kind of teacher is there?"

Her enthusiasm seemed forced. "Plenty," she was answering. "Gurus. Christian Scientists. I'm always meeting people who call themselves teachers—in my work."

"What kind of work do you do?" His voice was deliberately casual.

She ignored the question. "What do you teach? And where?"

He told her he taught English and social studies in a junior high school in Brooklyn. "I knew it!" she cried, again brimming over with enthusiasm. "I knew you weren't just a cabdriver. Do you teach school every day?"

"Yes."

"And drive a cab every night?"

"No. I'm sort of a relief man."

"What *is* your schedule?"

"I'm off and then I'm on for a couple of nights at a time." He paused.

She laughed. "Okay, David Marks." Her tone was gay and rather mocking. "At least I know your name and your address. It's right there on your license."

"Yeah."

"I like your picture—and I like your name," she said with more warmth and sincerity in her tone. "David. It's a fine old biblical name, isn't it?" Abruptly her voice grew sad. "I had a twin brother named David."

"No fooling."

"He died—in Vietnam."

"I'm sorry."

"And *I* lived," she said.

"I see you did." He glanced into the rear-view mirror, realizing all over again how beautiful she was, and wondering why anybody that beautiful could sound so bitter. "It should have been the other way around." She laid her head against the worn upholstery. She closed her eyes.

"You can drop me at the Barbizon-Plaza, if you don't mind," she said as they were crossing the Triboro Bridge in the rain. "And you *will* keep this quiet, won't you?"

Dave was silent.

"Please? Promise?"

"I don't see why it matters so much," he said. "If I don't know your name or who you are or how to find you, then you're just an anonymous woman passenger that I took up to Connecticut. So what's the difference—about the records?"

"The *address* would be there. Please. I'm asking it as a personal favor." They had stopped for a red light. She touched him lightly on the shoulder. "I won't ever ask you again. This is the last time. Please, David."

It was the first time she had called him David, but he swallowed for a second and then said, "It's not robbery, is it? You're not casing that place for a jewel heist?"

"Oh, my God." She laughed and slid her fingers off his shoulder. "You must look at a lot of television."

"I don't. I don't have time. How about spying?"

"Don't be silly." Again she laughed. "It's not anything like that."

"Then what is it?"

"Just please try not to worry. Or guess. You couldn't possibly guess it." She paused. She struck a match. "It's the last time anyway. I swear it. Do you promise?"

"Not to worry or not to record it?"

"Both." She laughed. The match went out.

"Okay," he finally muttered. "But if you ever ask me again, I'll *make* you tell."

"I will. I promise," she said softly.

When they reached the Barbizon-Plaza, she made no move to get out. "Would you mind pulling up past the entrance, please?"

she said. "I'm still so messy. I haven't even put my coat on." He pulled past the big lighted marquee of the Fifty-eighth Street entrance of the hotel, and she sat there, zipping up her boots and fiddling with her hair. "Is there any way I can get in touch with you," she asked, "aside from standing on that streetcorner and catching pneumonia?"

"Why would you want to?"

"Just to see you and talk to you."

The way she said it excited him. "Well, I'm in the phone book. David Marks. The Brooklyn phone book."

"No, I wouldn't want to call your home. When are you working again this week?"

"Wednesday and Thursday. Maybe Friday," he said. "You can always call me at the cab company. Just ask for Jim the dispatcher, tell him who you are and where you'd like me to pick you up."

"No, I wouldn't want to do that either," she answered quickly. "Why don't we think of some kind of signal?"

"Signal?"

"*I* know! I'll just say I'm your sister, I've gotten sick, it's an emergency." In the lights of Sixth Avenue she was looking at him with dancing eyes. "I'm in the hospital—then you can meet me at some place like the East Side Airlines Terminal."

"The East Side *Airlines* Terminal?"

"Yes. That would be ideal. That would work out just fine. Thank you so much, David."

She had unlatched the door. She was gliding out onto the sidewalk.

"Now wait a minute."

"Good night, David," she called.

Slender and graceful, with her long hair shining, she hurried up the street toward the entrance of the hotel. With umbrella dangling from her arm, skirts swinging above the boots she looked nothing like the bedraggled ghost who had appeared from the mist and rain of Red Mill Lane an hour ago. Just before she swept through the revolving doors of the hotel, she turned and smiled at him—a smile of dazzling promise.

And it was then Dave knew that he was head over heels in love with her—this girl whose name he still did not even know.

Five

There could be no other explanation for his past willingness to cooperate with her, and his obsessive behavior for the next couple of days. He had fallen in love with this beautiful, elusive girl, and was determined to find out all he could about her, probe the mystery she was involved in—and yet protect her secret at the same time.

He was acting like a churned-up schoolboy, a possessive lover, and it was more than mere idle curiosity by now. Dave's grief had made him extremely vulnerable to any form of human suffering. Obsessed with the cruel fate of his gentle young wife and idolizing her as a sort of martyr, he was ripe for any other young woman in trouble, particularly one who was sweet and refined and lovely—like Fran Marks.

Since her death he had lived the life of a hermit, a monk in a hair shirt. For six months he had not looked at a woman, much less gone to bed with one. Now all this pent-up energy was bursting into flame and threatening to consume him. Every reaction was exaggerated, every nuance, every word given special meaning in his mind.

The facts that the house was empty and that she wasn't a call girl helped considerably. So did her fierce reaction to the drug question. He could think of her from now on as pure and innocent, a wistful victim, a maiden he must rescue from the evil forces in her life. She had become a figure of fantasy who had no place in the drab routine of his days, his schoolteaching, or his nights behind the wheel of his cab.

Her mystery, her frail beauty, her air of glamour all added to her enchantment. So did that dark and splendid estate in which there never was a light and never a living soul. Everything about her fitted in with the unreal, dreamlike existence he had been living since his wife's death, the detachment and loneliness he had been feeling for the past six months.

Who she was and what she was involved in had to be something equally fantastic—and dangerous. "You'll never guess . . . don't try," she had said. But he was determined to know before another day went by.

From a sidewalk phone booth, shortly after he dropped her off at the Barbizon-Plaza, he phoned the Stamford directory assistance. There was a Philip E. Ferguson living on Red Mill Lane, but his number was unlisted.

On Forty-second Street near the subway station where Dave took the train home to Flatbush there was a large newsstand dealing in foreign and out-of-state periodicals. There, that same night, he bought a Stamford newspaper and on the way home he combed it. On a back page there was a brief item stating that a Sharon Ferguson of Red Mill Lane was visiting Portugal where she had recently taken a tour to the shrine of Fatima.

At school the next day during a study-hall period he phoned a Connecticut realtor whose ad was also in the Stamford paper. A woman answered.

"Good morning," he began. "My name is Sorenson and I'm calling about a house near Stamford on Red Mill Lane—a rather large estate. I think the owner's name is Ferguson."

"Oh, yes," she said. "A white one with a pond in front? And a rather long wooded driveway?"

"That's the one," he said. "It also has a tennis court."

"Yes," she said. "What did you want to know about it."

"I'm calling to ask if it's for sale," Dave replied, leaning against the finger-smudged wall of the shabby old school corridor. "If it is, I'd like to buy it."

"Oh, I very much doubt that it is," the woman said with a slight tremor in her voice. "What did you say your name was again?"

"Sorenson. I'm with the government. Jeremiah Sorenson."

She was silent for a moment. Then she said thoughtfully, "I

doubt it, Mr. Sorenson. It's been in the family for years and years, and I've never heard any mention of Mr. Ferguson wanting to sell."

"Could you ask him?" Dave said, picking a wad of chewing gum off the phone. "Would you be willing to transmit an offer?"

"He's in Florida right now," she said. "Deep-sea fishing. He goes down to the Keys nearly every winter."

Dave glanced toward the door of his classroom. Noise was rising from within. He could hear shouts, blows and the thunder of running feet. "Do you have any idea when he'll be back?" he asked.

"I think not for another couple of weeks," she said. "I could call someone, though I honestly don't think he'd even listen to almost any kind of offer at the moment." She cleared her throat. "But if you're interested in Connecticut properties, Mr. Sorenson, we have some other very attractive listings."

On Tuesday evening Mr. Kahn dropped in.

When Fran was a little girl, her mother had taken in roomers; some had remained Momma's lifelong friends. One was Mr. Joseph Kahn. A tiny man with sparse gray hair, he had been coming to Momma's house ever since Dave remembered, and now that she had moved in with Dave, he still continued to visit her. Momma always called him "Kahn." She treated him with casual indifference. But Fran had loved the gentle old man whom she had always called "Uncle Joe." And Dave liked him too. Since Fran's death he had been like a father to the young man.

It was Mr. Kahn, in fact, who had first suggested that Dave drive a cab "for therapy" after Dave's return from Bellevue. "Over my dead body!" Momma had objected when the idea was first broached. "That's a nudnik job. He's a schoolteacher—a professional man."

But looking at her over his glasses, Mr. Kahn had said in his mild voice, "I meant just as a sideline, Rose." Then, turning to Dave, he'd added softly, "Some men in your situation, son, they can ship out on a freighter, escape from everything. But you—you've got two children to think about. And it might help, if only to pass the time."

Dave's state of mind had been abysmal that November. He

28

was wandering the streets, unable to sleep or eat, or even to sit still in those first few weeks of his raw agony and rage.

"Think it over," Mr. Kahn said. "I can arrange it." Mr. Kahn, it appeared, could. Mr. Kahn, it seemed, "had connections." Although he lived in a furnished room and always wore the same gray suit, Mr. Kahn "knew people in the city," and in less time than one could imagine, Dave had a medallion and a job with a reputable cab company.

Cab-driving helped him. It had calmed him down and eaten up his energy. Mr. Kahn, however, shrugged off any thanks. "I didn't do anything," he insisted. "It was nothing." Mr. Kahn still preferred to be the perennial shadow, the humble guest who sat in Momma's living room, sipping innumerable glasses of tea or playing chess with Dave.

Even at chess he was equally modest. "Wonderful move, Dave. I don't see how I can avoid being beaten."

But he never was. He always won. And there were few problems that he couldn't seem to solve. After dinner on Tuesday, while Momma was putting the children to bed, Dave buttonholed him.

"Ever hear of a man called Philip Ferguson?"

The chessboard was set between them, the pieces all in place.

"Ferguson?" The old man looked up. "In what connection, son?"

"He lives in Connecticut near Stamford. An old family. Fishes a lot."

The old man shook his head.

"Never heard of him. I heard of a Homer Ferguson in Connecticut."

"What'd *he* do?"

"A real pirate. A bad actor." Mr. Kahn grimaced and moved his king's pawn. "He used to own a lot of textile mills back in the thirties."

"In Connecticut?"

"Somewhere around Bridgeport—or Danbury maybe. He made quite a name for himself anyway—with the unions," Mr. Kahn said. "He hired strikebreakers, roughnecks. There were heads smashed, and I think even a coupla killings. Why are you interested in him?"

"It's Philip I'm interested in," Dave replied. "Do you suppose they're related? Did he have any sons, this Homer Ferguson?"

"I don't know. I could find out. But why are you so interested?"

Dave shrugged. He studied the chessboard. Then he moved his queen's pawn. "One of the guys in the cab company," he said, "had a run-in with this man Ferguson. He made it sound like Philip Ferguson might have criminal connections . . ."

"So what's this to you?"

"Nothing. I was just curious. The driver's a friend of mine. There was some girl mixed up in it—some blonde or other—with Ferguson at the time."

"Hmm."

"Your move, Mr. Kahn." At that point Dave let the matter drop. He knew that he had said all he needed to say, and that in a day or two Mr. Kahn in a very casual way would come up with all Dave needed to know about Philip Ferguson's background and hopefully about his connection to the beautiful blond girl.

For it was the old man's style, a point of pride with him to research with a painstaking zeal any subject that took his fancy or came up in a conversation with Dave. Suggest an area of ignorance and he would come back with an encyclopedic report—on such far-ranging esoterica as Ivan Goncharov, John Jay, the Boxer Rebellion, Beethoven's deafness.

The old man moved a knight and took a small black notebook and a gold pencil from his vest pocket. In his spidery European-style penmanship he wrote "Philip Ferguson."

"Any middle initial?"

"E," Dave said.

The following evening Mr. Kahn again dropped by. Momma was upstairs visiting a neighbor, Mrs. Fox. After Dave had put the children to bed and put the kettle on for tea, the old man took out his notebook and laying it beside his glass said casually, "Your friend has nothing to worry about. He's not a criminal. He has no underworld connections. In fact, he's never done a day's work in his life."

"Philip Ferguson?"

"Philip *E.* Ferguson." The old man grinned. "The *E* stands for Emerson, a writer Homer Ferguson admired. And you were right, Dave. Homer had two sons, and Philip is the younger. A big disappointment to the old man, too, I would imagine."

"How so?"

"A real playboy, a good-time Charlie—who spends his time fishing or playing tennis," Mr. Kahn said. "He used to have a sailboat too. It was sixty-five feet long." He consulted his notebook. "It was called *The Rampage* and won lots of races. Isn't that a nice name for a boat?"

Dave smiled. He poured the tea.

"He shot a leopard in Africa," Mr. Kahn went on, peering at his notes. "He's fifty-four years old, a Harvard dropout and a Dartmouth dropout, in fact a dropout from at least six other colleges. But he didn't do too badly in the Navy in World War II. He got a medal for saving a crew member. Do you want me to go on?"

"How about the women, his personal life?" Dave asked.

Mr. Kahn's eyes twinkled. "In that regard he's a big success. A real ladies' man. He's had three wives, and two daughters by two different marriages. His latest wife, she's half his age."

"Is she a blonde?"

"No, dark-haired—part Russian. She was a script girl on a TV series when he met her in Chicago two years ago," Mr. Kahn said, "and he married her one week later."

Dave laughed. "You've sure done a job on him. Where did you dig all this up?"

"I've got sources," Mr. Kahn replied cryptically. He put the notebook back in his pocket. "I found him boring. A very dull man. But at least he doesn't sound dangerous. And you can tell your friend that." He stirred his tea. "He sounds too pleasure-loving to be dangerous . . . a real slob."

"Well, thank you," Dave said. "I'll tell my friend. And how about the girl?"

"What girl?"

"The blond girl I mentioned, the one the taxi driver saw him with. Did you find out anything about her?"

Mr. Kahn looked blank. "Was I supposed to?" he asked. Then he brightened. "No, but he loves blondes. He married two of them. And it could have been anyone of a hundred women, his daughters, his ex-wives, or just one of those airline hostesses he's always picking up."

Dave took a deep breath. "Well, thank you, Mr. Kahn. This has certainly been good of you."

"Don't mention it. It was nothing."

Six

At 8:15 on Thursday evening he was driving in from Kennedy Airport with two solemn black gentlemen in robes seated in the back seat of his cab when the dispatcher's voice came rasping through the speaker.

"Marks. Hey, Marks. Come in, Dave. I got a message for you."

"What's the message?"

"Your sister. She's sick. It's an emergency."

Dave felt his heart skip a couple of beats.

"You read me, Dave?" Jim the dispatcher rasped.

"Yeah, I read you." He flipped off the switch.

Talk of drought conditions and the United Nations resumed from the back seat.

He drove the two stately gentlemen to their hotel, helped them in with their luggage, and then headed for Thirty-seventh Street and the East Side Airlines Terminal.

She was standing close to the curb in the long black coat and boots, watching every cab that passed. The wind was blowing in wild gusts, wrapping the flowing coat around her body. Round her head was a black scarf, its ends whipping back and forth about her face. She looked pale, fragile, buffeted.

He drove past her, parking the cab halfway up the block close to Second Avenue. Then he got out and walked back.

"David!" She saw him and came running. In the light streaming from the terminal he could see the circles under her eyes. "I was so afraid you wouldn't come."

"Well—here I am," he said. "Can I buy you a drink?"

"I was afraid you wouldn't remember our signal." She hooked her arm through his, and then immediately withdrew it. "David, I'm afraid I'm going to have to break my word to you."

He trudged beside her in silence.

"I've got to be in Stamford. Just for half an hour this time."

"Nope."

He stopped and stood for a second with feet planted on the sidewalk. Then he turned and started walking back to his cab. She followed. "I told them I didn't want to. I refused to." Her voice was plaintive on the wind. "*Please*, David. I *have* to."

"Who is *them*?" He kept on walking. "Philip Ferguson? He's down in Florida."

"Listen—please. It's the last time—absolutely."

She flitted past him, opened the door of his cab and got into the back seat. From the shadows her eyes gazed up at him with a look of utter misery.

"Please, David. I'll kill myself," she whispered.

"Don't be ridiculous."

"I *will*." Her voice cracked.

He gazed up at the line of glittering skyscrapers etched against flying wind-clouds. Then he looked into the cab again.

"Why me?" he asked. "Why does it have to be me?"

In the shadows she turned her head away. Her hands twisted on her lap.

"The city is full of cabs," he said, "and guys who'd be glad to take you."

"No!"

"*Why?*"

"Because—" Her voice was a choked whisper.

"Because why?"

"Because *you're* the one I want." She raised the blue eyes to him with a wretched gaze. "The only one I trust. The only one who knows."

"Knows what?"

"About me. More than anyone . . . in the world." Her voice faltered. "No one knows as much about me—as *you* do, David Marks. And I swear I'll tell you the whole story if you'll take me up there now."

"Okay—then let's hear it."

"No." She drew back from him. "I meant—once it's over."

"Once *what's* over?"

"Please. It's getting so *late!*" With a panicky look she glanced out the cab window. Her fingers twisted the ends of the black chiffon scarf. "David, I swear—on the way back from Red Mill Lane, I'll tell you all of it. I promise to. I swear it—on the memory of my dead brother David."

For a long moment more he looked into the beautiful tormented eyes. Then he shook his head. "My God," he said softly. "You won't even tell me your name. What's your name? Tell me."

She lowered her eyes, twisted a button on her coat and took a deep breath. "It's Diana," she whispered.

"Just Diana?"

"Diana Roberts." She raised the big blue eyes. "Now, will you *please* take me? Please, David?" Her voice broke. "I can't delay a minute longer . . . it's a matter of life and death."

A lopsided moon raced them all the way to Stamford, flying in and out of windy, silvery-edged clouds. But when they reached Red Mill Lane, the moon had disappeared. The long hill was in deep shadow. Even the light of the church steeple had gone off.

"Look," he said, "the chain's down."

"Yes." Her voice was listless. As though she had spent her last ounce of energy persuading him to take her on this trip, she had sat in silence, chain-smoking, ever since they left the terminal.

"Let me drive you in," he said.

"No. Please stay here the same as always."

She got out slowly and stood beside his window, with the wind sweeping her coat wide and the ends of her scarf fluttering. "And please don't follow me tonight. Just stay here in your cab and wait. It isn't going to be long."

"How long?"

"Just half an hour, no more. I'll be back at quarter to eleven."

"If you're not, I'm coming after you."

"Don't. Be patient. *Please,* David."

Slipping her hand through the open window, she laid it lightly on his wrist. Her touch was cold. "Trust me," she whispered, stepping back and looking at him intensely. "And keep my secret."

"Diana."

She swept away from him like a leaf blown by the wind, and was gone, her slight figure melting into the darkness, her footsteps swallowed up by the wild rustling of the pines.

He waited for exactly half an hour. With arms folded, he sat stiffly, listening to the wind and looking at his watch. No one drove past him. The road was deserted. There were not even any lights on in the barn-red house up the hill. At exactly 10:45 he fixed his gaze steadily on the white gateposts. From far away he heard a truck or a bus grinding its gears uphill. At 10:50 he got out and started walking down the driveway.

The wind-tossed trees sang over him and the cold fresh breeze blew against his face. For a moment the moon appeared, and then went behind a cloud. The sky was pitch-dark when he reached the open lawn, the ruffled expanse of pond.

He stopped short, drawing in his breath.

A light was on in a downstairs window.

It was at the far left. All the rest of the house was in darkness. But in one window of one wing there was a dim glow, an unsteady flicker of light, as though a fire were lit inside. High above, from one of the tall chimneys, smoke trailed in wisps and then was blown in quick puffs against the misshapen face of the moon.

Dave moved closer.

He stared at the dark-red draperies, closely drawn and glowing faintly with flickering light. No shadow crossed them. Nothing moved except the light, which brightened, faded and brightened again as though flames were leaping on a hearth inside. Then something small and furry brushed his legs. He heard a plaintive meow.

It was a small black kitten. It rubbed against his legs, purring and meowing. As he stooped down, it frisked away, then waited, again meowing, its huge eyes glowing yellow in the dark. When he picked it up, it felt light and its neck was skinny in the circlet of blue beads. "Poor little bastard." It licked his fingers with a rough dry tongue.

He had some milk in a thermos bottle Momma had fixed for his midnight lunch, and he carried the kitten back to his cab. All the way to the gateposts it nestled in his arms, seemingly content to be stroked, but just as they were in sight of the road, it leaped, with a shrill meow, from his arms, and bounded off into the shadows with crooked little leaps, leaving him with a small scratch on his hand.

"Have you seen a black kitten?"

Out of the darkness an elderly woman in a sweater came toward him. With her was a little girl.

"Yes. It went that way." Dave pointed up the hill.

"Damn her." The old lady had white hair and a deep powerful voice. "Go look for her, Samantha."

"Here Inky, Inky." The child ran off and the old woman trudged after her. Their voices faded up the road. Dave turned back and went down the driveway. The light was still on in the house. The smoke still curled from the chimney. But there was no sign of Diana Roberts.

It was 11:05. He had waited an extra twenty minutes. He walked up the front steps to the front door and knocked.

The knocker was brass in the shape of an anchor. He lifted it and let it fall. Inside there was deep silence.

He let it fall three times. He pressed his ear close to the door. The light still glowed in the downstairs window. Smoke floated from the roof.

"Miss Roberts. Diana."

He tried the knob. It did not turn. He rapped and then hammered on the door. Running down the brick steps, he shouted.

"Diana!"

The wind hummed in the telephone wires, with a high keening, an eerie wail. The water sucked against the banks of the pond. Picking up a handful of wet gravel, he walked to the lighted window and tossed it against the glass. "Diana!" No response. The light inside grew dim, then bright. He began to circle the house, looking for other doors or an unlocked window.

Every door, every window was locked from the inside—except a Dutch door on the brick patio. Its upper half was loose and banging in the wind. Reaching inside, he found a key to the lower part and turned it. He walked in, and paused, listening to the echo of his own footsteps. "Diana?" His voice had a muffled sound. There was an odor of must, of rooms long shut up.

36

The walls felt cold and damp. The light switches didn't seem to be working.

"Diana . . . where are you?"

He could smell the fire.

Groping his way past staircases and doorways, he began to follow the scent of the smoke. The house was a maze of dead-end rooms and narrow hallways. He passed sheeted furniture, chandeliers in muslin bags, and a tiny table that toppled as he brushed by, and fell with a clatter and the crash of glass. Finally at the end of a long corridor he saw a chink of light under a door.

The smell of smoke was stronger. He could hear the fire's hiss and crackle. Pale shadows danced over mahogany and wallpaper as he paused, called her name again and knocked.

No answer.

He pushed the door open and walked in.

A fire blazed on a hearth, bookshelves lined the walls, and near the drawn crimson curtains a television set was on—without sound. Color images raced across the lighted screen in silence—a man riding a horse, an Indian warrior on a mountain peak. Near the fire were two high-backed chairs, a coffee table, a highball glass winking in the light of the leaping flames.

Dave's eyes were riveted on the carpet.

Stretched out on the floor, face down, lay the body of a gray-haired man. On his back, dark against the yellow shirt, was blood.

"My God!"

Toes down in tennis shoes, he lay motionless near one of the high-backed chairs. One thick, darkly freckled arm was extended toward the coffee table, as though he had tried to grasp it as he fell.

Dave dropped to his knees. He lifted the big limp hand. There was no pulse. The skin felt cold. It fell with a dull thud.

"God!" Then he noticed the small black string around the head.

Slowly he turned the body over.

Covering the left eye was a patch.

"DIANA!"

Dave's cry was now a howl, reverberating through the silent house.

Seven

It was six-thirty the next morning. He was in the kitchen, drinking water from a jelly glass. Momma shuffled in, wearing a pink hair net and a pink chenille robe. "For God's sake, Dave, what you doing up so early?"

"I couldn't sleep."

"*Again* you couldn't?" She looked him over skeptically. "You came home late enough," she said. "It was four in the morning."

It had been five. "Don't worry about it." Haggard and disheveled in the stained pants and sweaty windbreaker, he tried to sidle past her.

"You slept all night in your clothes? A real bum you're getting to be!" As he hurried down the hall, she called, "Where you going?"

"Out to get a paper."

"They're not even out this early. What do you want a paper for? You should get back in bed, Dave. I'm worried. You look terrible." Her voice followed him as he undid the chain bolt and went out.

Shivering in the cold gray light of dawn, he paced the sidewalk in front of the stationery store. When the truck appeared, he snatched up a copy of the *Daily News.* But there was nothing in the *News* about any murder in Connecticut.

Nor in the *New York Times* either. He plowed all the way through every section of the paper, fine-combing page after page as he walked back to the shabby yellow-brick apartment house. Nothing. It was too early, probably. Riding up in the self-service elevator, he folded the *Times* neatly and laid it surreptitiously in front of his next-door neighbor's apartment door. The *News* he kept for Momma.

All the familiar weekday noises of this ordinary Friday morning filled the air as he unlocked the door of his apartment and closed it quietly behind him. Radios and televisions were on, women were yelling and babies were crying—just as though the world had not caved in the night before.

The smell of coffee greeted him. The boys were up. He could hear their voices from the bedroom, then a patter of feet, a cry from Joel. "Grandma, Jeremy's wet his bed again!"

"Oh, my God!" he heard her grunt. He entered the back hallway just in time to see Jeremy toddling from the boys' room, thumb in mouth, the bottom of his Dr. Denton's soaked. "Bad boy!" Momma was running after him.

"Don't hit him. I'll take care of it."

He hastened to the familiar duties of fatherhood. Life was beginning again, and it was very real and earnest indeed. The bedding had to be stripped from the crib and soaked in the bathtub, Jeremy changed and suitably admonished, and Joel scolded for being a tattletale.

"But I never wet my pants when I was little, did I, Daddy?"

"Yes, you did, and you shouldn't tell on your brother."

"But now he'll have to wear his diapers again and rubber pants to bed."

Then Jeremy started crying and kicked his big brother in the shin. Yes, life was very real, and last night seemed a fantasy, a nightmare he had dreamed.

He sat with both children on his knees as the pale rays of morning filtered into the small cramped dinette, and he knew he hadn't dreamed it. Every detail was painfully real. The sun lit up the grease-spotted walls, the worn linoleum, the stove where Momma, with an apron over her bathrobe, was stirring oatmeal and frying eggs. It lit her sagging chin, her hunched old woman's shoulders. But he could still see that dead man looking up at him.

It was the man he had seen in the black convertible, the man who had killed Fran. Like a devil out of a nightmare, he had lain there on the dark red rug. Who the man was and how he had gotten there meant nothing in that moment of horror and recognition. Dave's search was over, fantastically, ironically. But it could not be coincidence. He had known that right away.

"Daddy, your mustache tickles." Joel giggled and wriggled on his lap.

"Yes, someday I'll shave it off."

"What's the matter with you?" Momma was staring at him again. "You lost your appetite? I fried them upside down especially." She took Jeremy off his lap. "Dave, honest to God, I never saw you looking so bad. It's no wonder with the life you live. Get off his lap, Joel darling. Your father's maybe got a virus."

"I'm okay. *Okay!* Just tired."

He stood under the shower for a long time, letting the hot water flow over him, until someone upstairs started knocking at the pipes. He washed his thick dark hair, trying to scrub away the stink of smoke and mildew, the unforgettable odor of that house. But as he dressed for school he could still smell it, smell the fire, and hear his voice echoing through that pitch-dark house. "Diana! *Diana!*" Yelling her name, he had run up and down stairs, opened doors and closets—like a man insane, a man still trying to convince himself that she was somewhere and would answer him.

Through the bright spring sunlight he walked, a tall young schoolteacher in a corduroy jacket. In the old gray school building bells clanged. Feet shuffled. Black faces, white faces, coffee-colored faces hurtled by, whooping in and out of classrooms he had to keep locked between bells.

He was running out into the wind and the roaring pine trees again, shouting for her through the trees and across the pond. He was racing around the pond and calling her name up the steep rocky slope rising to the dark red house above. "Diana! Diana!" Around the tennis court and down the railroad embankment he had raced, his voice hoarse against the wind. He had leaned out over the tracks, peering down, still calling, hearing the far-off whistle of a train. He had watched the train chug by.

"Mr. Marks, Jimmy's got a razor."

"Give me the razor, Jimmy."

"Aah, you filthy spick stoolie, I'm gonna cut your eyes out, I'm gonna chop you into little pieces."

He was deaf to the familiar din that filled his crowded classroom this morning. He scribbled on the blackboard like a sleepwalker. The eyes of Willie Moore were glazed with heroin. Dolores Sanchez' blouse was open, revealing her full breasts with nipples standing up. And the big boys in the back were looking, elbowing each other and guffawing. He could not cope today. He could not seem to concentrate. He was back in the front seat of his cab again, driving down winding roads past woods and sleeping settlements. At one in the morning he was walking into a railroad station, standing on an empty platform.

"Open your books, please—to page sixty-one."

He rapped on his desk. "Start reading." He pointed at random. "Gloria, you start."

"Me?" She giggled, wiggled her buttocks. The class guffawed. "Yes. *Start!*"

Clowning, still grinning, she rose. Moving a chipped orange fingernail slowly across the page of the tattered textbook, she began drawling the immortal lines,

> "Oh, what can ail thee, knight at arms,
> Alone and palely loitering?
> The sedge has withered from the lake,
> And no birds sing."

Every other word was mispronounced. She paused often to snicker and look around. She was thirteen years old, the daughter of a prostitute, and had been raped when she was seven. But Dave sat down. He nodded vaguely. His eyes drooped.

He was sitting slumped in his cab, half asleep, dead with exhaustion, driving back from Red Mill Lane—at three that morning. He was driving through the empty streets of Manhattan to Fifty-eighth Street and the silent entrance of the block-long Barbizon-Plaza Hotel.

Gloria faltered onward:

> "I met a lady in the meads,
> Full beautiful, a faery's child.
> Her hair was long, her foot was light,
> And her eyes were wild."

At four in the morning he was walking into the huge hotel lobby. A tired clerk yawned behind a counter. "Sorry," the man murmured, finally looking up from his files, "we have no Diana Roberts registered."

> "And there she lulled me asleep,
>   And there I dreamed—ah woe betide!
> The latest dream I ever dreamed.
>   On the cold hillside.
>
> "I saw pale kings and princes too
>   Pale warriors, death-pale were they all.
> They cried, 'La belle dame sans merci
>   Hath thee in thrall! ' "

The school bell clanged.

"Any calls for me, Momma?"

"No calls," she answered, when he phoned her at noon. "So who were you expecting?"

At the cab company the day dispatcher had received no messages either. And in the late edition of the *Times* and an early edition of the *Post* there was no word of any murder on Red Mill Lane in Stamford, Connecticut. Nor was there any mention on the radio or the TV.

He lay in the empty flat with the radio on, watching the afternoon light flow and retreat around Fran's white curtains and the shadows of the fire escape. Momma had taken the boys to the playground. From below, in the courtyard, kids were playing ball and shouting. The sounds echoed up through the yellow-brick walls and floated in through the unscreened windows. It was warm, a sunny spring day, and he kept visualizing that book-lined library, that white house and that long driveway lined with pines. He kept seeing the light fading from the pond and the lawn and withdrawing from the drawn red curtains. From the rug, the highball glass and the motionless freckled hand it would gradually retreat, leaving the room dark, with only the television set still on. With its screen still glowing, its images still flickering silently, the TV would go on broadcasting show after show . . . to that dead man on the floor.

He squirmed on the white chenille spread. He got up, and walking to the phone in the living room, sat down and picked up the receiver. *"Trust me. Keep my secret."* He could hear her voice clear as crystal in his ears. He could feel her ice-cold touch. He laid the phone back on the cradle, poured himself some rye, and lay drinking it, staring at the light retreating from the stained ceiling of his bedroom. Putting the empty glass down, he punched the pillow into a ball. He buried his face in it.

That night he drove his cab up the street of desolate warehouses. He cruised around the neighborhood of the Barbizon-Plaza Hotel and the Fifty-seventh Street subway station. Almost twenty-four hours had passed since he had walked into that empty house, and barely a week had gone by since he had first laid eyes on her. But his life was totally changed. It could never be the same again. Fear had entered it, and creeping evil. A frightful gift had been given him—a wish fulfilled—but at what cost?

Eight

Mr. Kahn's furnished room was in the back of an old frame house in Bensonhurst. The front was occupied by a dentist, and as Dave climbed the stairway he could hear a drill going and see the dispirited faces of several patients ranged around the green walls of a waiting room.

He knocked on a door that was sticky with fresh varnish.

"Come in, son." Mr. Kahn greeted him in shirt sleeves and shabby gray vest. The room was full of sunlight. Huge, immaculately clean, but sparsely furnished, it had a large old-fashioned bay window overlooking a backyard.

Two chairs were set in front of the window, and beyond the sparkling pane a tree with snow-white blossoms was bursting into bloom. Birds fluttered around a bird feeder set on a window ledge.

"Sit down, Dave. Coffee?"

"Thank you."

In one corner was a hot plate and above it two shelves of foodstuffs and dishes. Socks hung on a string above a washbowl. For a man with "connections," Mr. Kahn lived very austerely indeed. There were no books or pictures in sight, only a battered desk with a phone on it, and on the old-fashioned bureau a small gold-framed photograph of a woman and a little boy. The woman wore dark braids wrapped around her head and the little boy was dressed in a white sailor suit.

"So what brings you here?" Mr. Kahn was bringing coffee in two chipped mugs. "You sounded very upset on the phone."

"I am."

Mr. Kahn sat down in the platform rocker set before the bay window. "So tell me." He blew on his coffee.

"It's crazy. I don't know what to do about it." Dave leaned forward in the Morris chair, facing Mr. Kahn. "I found that man who killed my wife."

"You—what?"

"The hit-and-run driver."

"Oh, my God."

Mr. Kahn's coffee cup rattled. He slopped coffee on his trousers.

"But dead," Dave said quickly. "Murdered." And then in full detail he told Mr. Kahn all the events of the past few days—his encounter with the girl who called herself Diana Roberts, the three rides to Stamford, and the fantastic shock of finding the very man he had been seeking for six months shot dead in an empty house.

With intent gaze the old man listened. "And you have told the police nothing?" he asked, when Dave was done.

"Nothing. You're the first to know."

"And there's been nothing in the papers?"

"Nothing—as far as I know."

"Hm." The old man stroked his chin.

Feet dangling above the parquet floor, coffee mug balanced on one knee, he sat in deep thought. Finally he asked, "Dave, you're sure it was the same man?"

"Mr. Kahn, it happened. It was real," Dave said. But the old man raised his hand.

"I'm not talking about that. I believe you," Mr. Kahn said. "I'm just asking—how can you be sure it was the same person you saw for just a couple of minutes from a distance on that night six months ago?"

Dave frowned.

"You were struck down by the car, remember—from behind. You were knocked out cold," Mr. Kahn continued. "You had only one quick look at him before you blacked out on the sidewalk, isn't that right, son?" He looked anxiously at Dave. "Yet now you think you recognize him for sure when he's lying on his back, dead, in a room lit only by a fire six months later." The rocker creaked. "So I'm asking you—are you positive it's the same man?"

Dave thought for a few seconds, again visualizing that firelit room and that hawklike face with its black eye patch. The other eye had been open, the lid drooping with a cynical expression. Even in death the face seemed to mock him, jeer at him, as though the man were still alive—and finding him ridiculous.

"Well?" Mr. Kahn was asking.

"I'm sure that it was he," Dave said in a low voice. "It was a face that was one in a million. A horrible face. You could never forget it."

"All right. I just wanted to make sure."

"I'm sure."

Mr. Kahn rose from the platform rocker. A small slight figure with wispy gray hair and rimless glasses sliding down his nose, he walked to the window and stood looking out at the white tree. Then he turned and looked sadly at Dave. "That makes it very simple, doesn't it?"

"Yes."

"If it's the same man you were looking for, then you've been used," Mr. Kahn said slowly. "They set you up for a fall guy—framed you. That's what those three trips were all about, son—to get you into that empty house with the body of a man you hated so they could pin the murder on you."

"I know. I realize."

Dave slumped unhappily in the Morris chair.

"May I ask you a couple of questions?" Mr. Kahn perched on the window sill.

"Go right ahead."

"When this girl first came along," Mr. Kahn said, looking at him over his spectacles, "didn't it ever occur to you that it was a little fishy, the whole thing?"

Dave shrugged. "Not particularly—at first."

"But such a bad street," Mr. Kahn persisted, "and so close to the garage? Her looking in the window at you as though to check you over? And having the money all ready. It didn't seem to you—arranged?"

"Not really," Dave replied. "I was just glad to have the job—and the money ahead of time."

"And the second night?"

"The second night I wasn't too happy about it, but it was raining cats and dogs, and I couldn't leave her on the street."

Mr. Kahn was studying him intently. Mr. Kahn was pursing up his lips.

"It was the third time I really should have said no," Dave said. "And I did. I tried. I even asked her why it had to be me."

"And what did she answer?"

"She said because she could trust me. She said she'd kill herself if I didn't take her up there. It was a matter of life and death."

"Hah!" Mr. Kahn said. "She knew it had to be you or the scheme would never work."

"I suppose so," Dave said glumly. "But that's all after the fact, Mr. Kahn. How could I possibly have guessed what she was up to?" He stared bleakly into space. "I'm not sure even now . . ."

"What do you mean?"

"I don't know what happened to her that night—whether she's dead—or—or how she got away."

Mr. Kahn said nothing. He gazed at the ceiling. As Dave stared at him, he turned his eyes back to Dave, cleared his throat and smiled awkwardly. "Let's go on, son. After you found the body, then what did you do?"

"Called her. Started looking for her."

"Why? Because you thought she had shot him?"

"I didn't know who had shot him."

"But you saw no one else?"

"No one."

"He was still bleeding?"

"Yes," Dave said.

"Not stiff yet?"

"No."

"You heard no shots fired?"

"Nothing. But the wind was making plenty of noise. Doors were banging. Branches were falling."

Mr. Kahn moved from the bay window. "Let's return to the moment after you found him. Was there a phone in that library?"

"I think so. Yes. On a desk in a corner."

"But you didn't go near it?"

"No."

"Why?"

"I don't know why." Dave felt his face beginning to burn. "I guess I—just panicked. I went nuts for a while. I just wanted to find her and get the hell out of there."

"But why did you want to find her?" Mr. Kahn continued to press. "Didn't you realize she had double-crossed you?"

Dave was silent.

"Or didn't you want to think that?" Mr. Kahn asked.

Dave rose from his chair. He rubbed his palms together. "I guess I didn't want to think it." He turned away, staring gloomily across the big bare room. "Look. I know I've done everything wrong. I've been a fool, an easy mark, a pushover. I haven't used my head."

"Yes." Mr. Kahn's lips barely moved. He gazed down at the worn parquet.

"I've even messed you up, bollixed that cab job you got me." Dave paced up and down. "Lied about the trip sheets. Broke the law. Faked the addresses."

Mr. Kahn's hand came down on his shoulder. "Dave," he said softly. "Stop it, stop blaming yourself. "What's done is done. You did what your heart thought best. And the heart, it is important. It does not always make sense . . . the heart."

As Dave looked at him, he broke off. He was looking at the picture on the bureau. Then he walked away toward the narrow white bed with its old-fashioned quilt and its cheap bedside lamp. When he turned and spoke again, it was in a voice choked with emotion.

"Once I lost—two people in my life," he said. "And only then did I become intelligent. I could play games, solve problems— and make money. But there was no heart left in me. The heart was gone."

Mr. Kahn had never talked about his past to Dave. But now he began to speak in broken phrases, his delivery breathless, his eyes overbright and his face flushed.

"I was even able to destroy," he said. "I knew the meaning of revenge." He paced up and down beside the bed. "The man who killed them I found. The guard in the gas chamber." He gestured toward the picture of the child and the young woman. "But I did not kill him. I undermined him so that he never knew what I had done. I *forced* that monster to commit suicide."

With clouded gaze he glanced at the bay window and, smiling sadly, tapped his wrinkled forehead. "Yes, I learned the secrets of the mind," he muttered, his eyes feverish. "Deduction. Strategy. And—cunning."

Suddenly he seemed to sag, and he looked at Dave with infinite wistfulness. "But it was no good, son. No life inside me any more."

He sank into the platform rocker, and waved his hand toward the drab furniture, the bare white walls. "Better to have the heart, Dave." The mood was passing and his voice grew calmer. "I was afraid last year that you might lose all feeling for life and people. But this proves you haven't."

"Yes."

"Don't lose the heart, son," Mr. Kahn said softly. "Ever . . . More coffee?"

"I'll get it."

"Thanks, Dave."

As Dave poured the coffee, he could hear the creak of the platform rocker and see the old man's face turned toward the waning light. The shadows of birds passed across the pane and their soft cooing sounded from the feeder.

"So—what to do about the situation."

Mr. Kahn put down his coffee cup and set his small feet on the floor. "The mind now, not the heart. What's the next step? That's the question."

"Should I report it or not?" Dave asked.

"Report it?" Why?" The old man quavered. He looked alarmed.

"Well, the longer I wait the worse it's going to seem—from the police standpoint, that is. And aside from that, it's probably my duty."

"Duty, duty. Phooey, duty."

Sputtering, shrugging, Mr. Kahn rose from the rocker. "Don't worry about duty, my son." He advanced to Dave. "Think only about yourself, your situation. *Somebody* will find that good-for-nothing in Connecticut, and who cares how long he's got to rot there." He frowned. "But *you* talk to the police, and they'll know right off the bat you were up there in that house, you were in the room that night with the body."

Mr. Kahn circled the Morris chair. "You identify yourself for *free,*" he sputtered, "and right away you become a suspect." He jabbed a finger into thin air. "Maybe that's what the real murderer wants from you, what the person who framed you is hoping for. That you'll report the body, and hence automatically turn yourself in. It was *expected* you would report it, probably— so the rest would be very easy . . . a perfect alibi."

Dave sat staring at him in the gathering dusk.

"But if you *don't* report it," Mr. Kahn continued, still circling round his chair, "if you keep quiet and play dumb, then somebody *else* has got to report it, and somebody *else* has got to prove that you were there. Right, son?" His old gray eyes were glittering. "And that's a longer, harder business, Dave, so"—he smiled triumphantly for a second—"so maybe your instinct or heart was right."

"I don't altogether understand."

"In protecting the girl, you protected yourself," said Mr. Kahn in his soft dry voice. "So now, all you are is simply some unknown cabdriver whom a coupla people might have seen outside that property that night. But unless one of them took down your license number, there are maybe eighteen or twenty thousand like you, driving taxis in New York."

"But supposing somebody did take down my license number. Or the murderer decides to phone it to the police—"

"That we'll face when we get there," Mr. Kahn said. He stopped pacing and turned on a lamp. "Meanwhile we've got some time, son, and time is very important—for our own investigation."

"Our own investigation?"

"Of course. You think we're going to *wait* for everything to happen, take it lying down, like a coupla doormats?"

"But how could I find out anything, without laying myself wide open? They're in Connecticut—and I'm down here."

"The usual way," Mr. Kahn said quietly. "Get yourself a detective."

"I couldn't afford any detective."

Mr. Kahn straightened up. He pushed his glasses up on his nose. He beamed.

"*I'll* be your detective!"

"Mr. Kahn!"

"I mean it. So what's the matter with me? I have the time—plenty of it—and I'm no slouch when it comes to investigation."

"Mr. Kahn." Dave rose to his feet. "That's very kind of you, but I couldn't possibly let you." The old man was seventy-two and had a history of heart disease. But waving a disparaging hand and shaking his head, Mr. Kahn walked briskly to the bureau and pulled open a drawer.

"Listen, you can't go up to Connecticut yourself, Dave. It's risky. They'd recognize you," Mr. Kahn said as he drew the notebook and gold pencil from under a pile of clean underwear. "From now on what you've got to do is stay out of the picture altogether, lay low, stay quiet as a mouse." He slammed the drawer shut. "And I'll do all the legwork, the traveling, the interviewing." He seemed delighted at the prospect.

"Yes, but these are terrible people. Criminals," Dave said.

"You think I'm not familiar with criminals?" Again Mr. Kahn glanced at the sweet-faced woman and the little boy. "Listen, my son, it would be a pleasure, a great privilege to destroy that filthy swine who thought up such a scheme—so vile, so diabolical a trick. A real pleasure."

He sat down.

Then opening the notebook and unscrewing the gold pencil, he began to write down everything that Dave had told him.

Nine

Bright and early the next day Mr. Kahn set off for the city of Stamford by train. But he had scarcely gotten off the New York, New Haven and Hartford railroad when the news broke. The headlines greeted Dave when he left school at lunchtime and checked his favorite newsstand on Nostrand Avenue.

CONNECTICUT SPORTSMAN SLAIN. PHILIP FERGUSON FOUND DEAD IN LIBRARY OF HIS ESTATE NEAR STAMFORD. Accompanying the story was a picture of the dead man. The face was the same hawklike face he had seen glaring at him in the light of a dying fire. Ferguson, the owner of the house. The man Mr. Kahn had already done some research on. The playboy. The deep-sea fisherman. The husband of three wives. And the man Diana Roberts had said she knew nothing about.

He was dead. His body had been found in the library of his palatial home. And the newspapers were making a big thing of it. Murder is always good copy, particularly when it happens to the rich and venal. Philip Ferguson had been both, and for the next few days all the unsavory details of his life would be covered with appropriate relish by the news media. Millions of Americans would read about his escapades, his extravagances and the beautiful women in his life. He had been flamboyant, restless, ruthless, and endowed with a strangely compelling charm. He had lived like a prince of old. Women had adored him; men had despised and envied him. A superb athlete, a man of rugged strength and a curious sardonic ugliness, he had never lacked self-confidence or wavered from the belief that the world was his to enjoy. In the past few months, the papers said, his health had not been altogether perfect. He had suffered from gout and occasional back trouble. But just the same he had gone off to Florida, deep-sea fishing, as he usually did in the early spring, and caught six marlin of record size before his death.

Dave and Mr. Kahn devoured everything. They sat hypnotized reading all manner of newspapers and discussing them in delicatessens, Brooklyn bars or in Mr. Kahn's furnished room in Bensonhurst. Rehashing every item, speculating on every point, they walked up and down Flatbush Avenue, arguing and gesticulating. They sat pondering on dusty benches under the blighted trees of Eastern Parkway or overlooking the great Sheep Meadow of Prospect Park.

From day to day, from hour to hour, they kept waiting for the name of Diana Roberts to be mentioned. They kept waiting with baited breath for any reference to David Marks . . .

Ferguson's third wife, Sharon Ferguson, had discovered the body on her return home from Portugal. She was twenty-seven years old, a former beauty contest winner and TV script girl from Cicero, Illinois. Twenty-seven years younger than her fifty-four-year-old husband, she had been married to Ferguson for about two years. There had been no children. Three weeks before the murder they had left Connecticut on separate vacations, he to go fishing aboard his luxurious cabin cruiser in the Gulf of Mexico and she to take a tour of Portugal, including a trip to Fatima. She was a Baptist.

"Phil liked to fish but it made me seasick," she told police. "I told him just to go on down to Florida this year, and I'd look after myself. He didn't care for Europe any more. He said he'd seen it in its best days, and was bored with sightseeing."

They had kept in touch by phone. He had called her twice a week, over a transatlantic connection, made from different ports along the Gulf. He was fishing alone this year, with only two Mexican boys as crew, but she did not worry about him when he failed to call her that final week. "I figured he was having fun or too busy fishing to come into port often. Besides, I was moving around a lot, and perhaps he had failed to reach me."

She left Lisbon on schedule and arrived by jet at 8:00 P.M. Sunday evening at Kennedy.

"Phil was due back from Florida the following Tuesday," she told police.

The travel agency had arranged for her to be driven up to Stamford in a limousine Sunday evening, but at the last minute the limousine was unavailable, and she had rented a car and driven to the house on Red Mill Lane herself.

She had arrived there at approximately 9:30 P.M.

"I noticed nothing unusual," she told police. "The chain was up across the driveway just as Phil and I had left it three weeks ago, and I had to get out of the car and unfasten it before I could drive in." The house was dark, she reported, the front door locked, and the interior cold. "We had turned off the heat and the electricity when we left home." She went to turn on the master switch, and when the light illumined the front hall, she noticed a small overnight bag lying on a chair near the staircase. "It was my husband's."

She ran upstairs and looked for him.

In the master bedroom she noticed that the bedclothes were in disarray. Her husband's watch and some loose change lay on a chest of drawers. A bathroom faucet was dripping and some damp towels lay on the floor of the glass shower stall. "By this time I was quite sure he had come home ahead of time, though I couldn't imagine why. He hadn't turned on the lights and the heat. I went downstairs again. He had eaten something in the kitchen. There was a pot half full of tomato soup on the kitchen counter and some saltine crumbs on the kitchen floor. I kept walking around expecting him to appear. I called him outside the house. I noticed that the Dutch door leading to the terrace was ajar."

On the carpet inside the Dutch door she also noticed a couple of dusty footprints, male footprints. They led from the Dutch door down the hallway. She smelled stale wood smoke. The library door was open.

"I called him again. As I got closer to the library I saw a peculiar light flickering from inside the room. When I looked in, I saw that the television set which runs on a battery was on, but the sound seemed to be turned off. I walked across the room and stumbled over something. It was my husband's body."

Ten minutes later, in the home of Robert Trench, a neighbor, his young Canadian secretary, Margaret Carson, was typing a manuscript when she heard screams coming from the Ferguson property. She ran out to investigate. "Mrs. Ferguson was coming up the hill toward me, very distraught," Miss Carson reported. "She told me that her husband had been shot and his body was lying in a pool of blood on the floor of their library."

Miss Carson notified the police at once. But neither she nor her employer, a forty-five-year-old writer and close friend of Philip Ferguson's, had heard anything unusual from the neighboring property. No shots. No sounds of violence. "I didn't even know Phil was back," said Robert Trench. "He hadn't phoned me, and I hadn't seen him."

None of the other neighbors had heard anything unusual either. But then, as the newspapers pointed out, the house lay far back from the road behind a long winding driveway of evergreens. It was surrounded by at least ten acres of land. "Almost anything could have happened in that isolated spot," said one reporter, "and no one out there on the road or around the corner would have been any the wiser. The nearest house was at least a thousand feet away."

Philip Ferguson had been shot in the back with a .22-caliber bullet. The medical examiner who performed the autopsy estimated that he had been dead for approximately three days when Mrs. Ferguson found him. Thus the date of the murder was established, quite accurately, as the evening of March 31, and the time was thought to be sometime between ten in the evening and midnight.

"*Very* good," said Mr. Kahn. "Modern science is wonderful." And he sipped another glass of tea in a spa called Manny's Delicatessen.

On the morning of March 31 Philip Ferguson was still alive. The police traced his movements and found that at ten o'clock that day he had come ashore at Islamorada, Florida, in his fifty-foot cabin cruiser, *Siren Song*, berthing it at a marina he had never used before.

Saying nothing to the two Mexican boys about his plans, he had dismissed them both, given the keys of his boat to the marina owner, and left by cab for Miami Airport. The man at the marina recalled that he was wearing a yellow shirt, gray slacks and tennis shoes, and he was carrying a small overnight bag. Tossed over one shoulder was a madras jacket and over his left eye was a black patch.

"I remember him," the man at the marina told the police. "He gave me an extra twenty dollars, and asked me to hose down his boat for him. He said he'd be back in a couple of days."

A flight manifest for a jet leaving Miami for New York at 11:30 A.M. on March 31 had Philip Ferguson's name listed, and a blond stewardess in first class remembered him as "the man with the black patch who made a pass at me." She had served him three martinis and smiled politely when he stroked her leg. "He said he'd love me to have dinner with him, on his boat, when he got back to Florida."

The plane arrived at Kennedy at 4:10 P.M. on Thursday afternoon. But after Kennedy the trail ended. No parking-lot attendant remembered seeing a man with a black eye patch, no airport bus driver or car rental agent. Somebody had obviously met him and driven him to Stamford, Connecticut, but who that somebody was the police could not discover. And why Ferguson had returned, what had induced him to interrupt his Florida vacation, and what he had been doing in that house between the time he put his overnight bag down in the front hall and was shot in the back while drinking Scotch and looking at television before the fire in his chilly library, no one could tell either.

He had made no phone calls, not one from the Stamford house.

Nor had he received any.

In New York, from the airport, he had called no member of his family—not his older brother Alexander, none of his ex-wives, nor his two daughters. He had called nobody at the textile company, not his lawyer, his banker, nor his stockbroker —nor anyone on his limited list of friends.

Silently, circumspectly, this man who was by nature arrogant and impulsive had secretly returned home, taken a shower, fixed himself some soup, perhaps lain down for a few moments, swallowed a couple of aspirin, and then walked downstairs to build himself a fire, fix himself a drink and wait before his television set for Death to walk in.

But who was Death?

Who had summoned Ferguson and who had shot him?

That the police did not yet know.

And neither did Dave or Mr. Kahn.

*   *   *

However, it was only a matter of time before the "New York cabdriver" was played up by the press.

He had been seen "lurking about" the Ferguson gates, the papers said, for two or three nights previous to the crime and also on the established night of the murder itself.

A boy of fourteen, Charles Miller of Redding Center, had spied him while bicycling home from a school basketball game on the night of March 24, a week before the murder.

Riding down Red Mill Lane at approximately nine-fifteen on that moonlit Thursday, young Miller had passed a tall dark young man in a tan windbreaker walking down the road. Nearby was a yellow cab, parked in front of the Ferguson driveway. "The guy had a black mustache," said Miller, "and lots of thick hair. He was about six feet tall. The cab wasn't local. It had New York license plates."

A tall dark-haired young man had also been seen that same night by Robert Trench, the writer.

"I had been to Westport to a movie," Trench said, "and the headlights of my car picked out this person walking down Red Mill Lane. He was a tall, well-built young man with shaggy dark hair and a dark mustache. He was shabbily dressed, and was trudging down the hill toward a yellow cab parked at the head of Phil Ferguson's driveway. I offered him a lift, but he refused. The cab was empty. Its lights were off and its engine wasn't running. He seemed quite startled to see me."

"Who wouldn't be startled?" Dave said. "He turned his headlights full on me."

Mr. Kahn shrugged. He turned the pages of the Bridgeport newspaper. "Be glad he didn't take down your license number. That's the only thing important."

They read on.

As the rain poured outside the bay window, scattering the white petals of the flowering pear tree, they read about the rest of the "eyewitnesses." It was like looking at oneself in a fun house mirror at Coney Island. It was a completely absurd interpretation of completely innocent behavior. Yet Dave realized that everything he had done during those hours of waiting in Connecticut could be regarded as suspicious.

Without a passenger in sight, he had seemed to have no purpose there. The house was empty. All the neighbors knew it.

The chain was up. Yet for a good hour he had parked there at the head of that dark driveway and loitered around the property. He had spoken to no one, deliberately avoided speaking—as Diana had asked him to. And no one, obviously, not one single neighbor or guest at that party had laid eyes on Diana the whole time.

He had protected her to the letter.

And she had protected him not at all.

"Muffin," the girl in the yellow slicker, and her drunken boyfriend were not mentioned in the reports, but Mrs. Harriet Shaw was, and the police seemed to think that her testimony was vital.

She was the elderly lady in the sweater with the deep voice and the little granddaughter named Samantha. She said she had seen the tall dark young cabdriver, even talked to him—on the night of the murder.

"It was sometime between ten and eleven. I was looking for my lost kitten. As I came abreast of the Ferguson driveway," said Mrs. Shaw, "I saw this dark shadow walking toward me. He was coming out of the pine trees. He wore a tan windbreaker. He had a mustache and a Brooklyn accent. He seemed very nervous and very anxious to get rid of me."

Dave let the newspaper slide to the floor.

"That does it," he said. "It's all over."

"Nonsense. It doesn't say she took down your license number," Mr. Kahn said from the platform rocker. "And there are still eighteen thousand of you."

"Not eighteen thousand with mustaches and Brooklyn accents."

"Well, you can always shave it off."

Dave got up restlessly.

Mr. Kahn rocked, watching him. "They don't even know that Ferguson killed Fran yet," Mr. Kahn said softly. "That's all got to come out in the wash too, Dave—before they can even begin to hang it on you."

"Yes, but if they catch me first, they'll know all about Fran automatically." Dave stood glowering at the rain for a moment. Then he turned. "God, Mr. Kahn, I'm beginning to feel like such a fink-out. All this hiding, this waiting. Pussyfooting. Letting *you* do the work."

58

"Sure, but what do you want, son?" Mr. Kahn's feet hit the floor. "Better you should pussyfoot than stick your neck out for that murderer!" He looked at Dave sharply. "Listen—you go to the police now, you have no proof she even existed. And you don't. They'll say you went into that house, that library on your own, believe me. You drove up there all by yourself."

"But that's ridiculous. I can convince them—"

"Without the trip sheets? With the fake addresses?" Mr. Kahn's fingers tightened on the arm of his rocking chair. "How can you prove you ever had a passenger? Dave, it was all figured out ahead of time."

He rose. His face was flushed. His gray head trembled. "Son, please don't panic. You go to the police now, you haven't got a chance." He laid small shaking fingers on Dave's arm. "At this stage, those detectives, they're dying to find a suspect, somebody they can pin it on—and they can always say you're crazy, you're insane with grief since your wife died." He paused a moment. "You were in Bellevue, remember. And you made a statement to the police. Do you recall that statement?" he asked softly.

"Yes, of course I do."

"Well—all they need is to get hold of it," said Mr. Kahn, turning from him and moving back to his rocker. "Please just be patient, son. It's your best weapon." He gestured toward the Morris chair. "We're making progress . . . and meanwhile you have no address for her, no way to find her. In the eyes of the world there never was a Diana Roberts."

"Okay." Dave eased himself down on the old black leather upholstery. "Where do you suppose she is, actually?"

"Probably in Bermuda," Mr. Kahn replied dryly. "On some nice beach getting herself a tan."

Ten

It was dusk. The sun was sinking. Unbeknownst to Mr. Kahn, Dave had sneaked up on the bus, and now he stood on the green lawn of the white church, looking down the long steep slope of Red Mill Lane. He wore sunglasses, a cap and a dark raincoat. Unable to rest or stay in New York another moment, he had come up after school to see what he could see.

Everything was quiet. Everything looked peaceful, normal. Two days before, Philip Ferguson had been buried. His funeral had taken place in this quiet little church that overlooked his home. The road, according to Mr. Kahn, had swarmed with cars and people and state troopers—but no girl answering the description of Diana Roberts had appeared. Now it was deserted, tranquil. Nothing moved. No cars ground up the hill. And in front of the Ferguson gateposts far below, where for three nights his taxi had waited, there was no one, merely the grassy shoulder of the road and the shadows of the towering pines.

Above his head the cross on top of the church steeple caught the last rays of dying light, and in the gladed churchyard at his feet the old tombstones cast long bent shadows on the lawn.

He kept moving, looking down.

He was seeing it in daylight, seeing it in color for the first time.

And he was seeing it from a different perspective—from the top rather than from below.

From this high hill he could look down almost like an eagle from an aerie into the Ferguson estate and see it all spread out before his eyes. He could see it totally, the line of pine trees along the drive, the pond, the house, and see it diminished, as though it were a toy estate in a cardboard box, with tiny trees and a bit of mirror for a pond.

There, slightly to the left, was the wooded rocky slope, sharp with jutting granite ledges, up which Mrs. Ferguson had climbed after discovering her husband's body. And there, perched halfway up this rise, was the barn-red house with its flagstoned terrace and low curving stone wall where Robert Trench lived. It had a silo looming at one side, and looked very much like an old stable.

Smoke curled from its single chimney. A lady's bicycle leaned against a wall. A cat was cleaning its whiskers on the terrace. But that was all that was of interest in the Trench house at the moment.

Dave's eyes moved on downward to the blue pond—intensely blue in the fading light—and to the white house, like a huge dollhouse with its steep roofs and blackened chimneys, and to the library, the far wing, where Ferguson's body had lain.

Curtains, darkly crimson, floated and ballooned out through the open windows. And from the chimney directly above this room, smoke curled lazily against the sunset sky.

He watched. He noted every detail.

A small red sports car with the top down was parked in front of the foot of the brick steps. Behind it was a white station wagon and behind that was a Rolls-Royce. Parked at right angles to the pond at a distance from these other cars was a truck piled with dirt and flowering bushes.

Life down there in the Ferguson mansion seemed to be moving on apace.

For now, as Dave watched from his post high up the hill, a figure in blue jeans appeared, trundling a wheelbarrow. In the wheelbarrow were potted geraniums, looking tiny as red fingernails from this distance. The figure was slender, stoop-shouldered, with long dank brown hair. Moving round the side of the house it disappeared, and then a few minutes later reappeared, trundling the empty wheelbarrow back to the greenhouse.

The light was going.

Dave kept straining his eyes.

A lamp went on in a downstairs window, and then another,

and another. Suddenly the front door opened and a doll-sized woman in a long lavender robe stood silhouetted against the square of light streaming from the door.

She moved forward and went slowly, gingerly, down the shallow brick steps.

A tiny puppet in flowing violet draperies with a mane of dark hair that shadowed her averted face, she descended to the grass, holding up her long skirts. Then, dropping them, she trailed slowly toward the pond and stood beside it, looking down at the water.

"Sha–ron!"

A thin faint voice floated from a distance. And the dark-haired woman turned. She gazed toward the greenhouse, where a dim light had just gone on. Slowly she began to walk toward it, her draperies trailing across the grass.

But Dave's eyes had already been distracted elsewhere.

He was peering down through the twilight at a blond figure who had just stepped out of the pine trees.

For a moment he thought he had seen a ghost—the ghost of Diana Roberts . . .

"Looking for someone?"

He had not heard the man approach. He had heard nothing, so intent was he on the ghostly vision below. But the man was right behind him. He had come from somewhere along the road. His voice was vaguely familiar. "I live here," the man said pleasantly. "And I'd be glad to help you."

Dave put his sunglasses back on. Slowly he turned his head.

The man was the same fair-haired chap he had glimpsed in the Thunderbird that first night, the man who had offered him a lift. He was Robert Trench, the writer.

Tonight he was on foot. He wore a dark-green warm-up suit and carried a tennis racket.

"I was just waiting for the bus," Dave said.

"Oh? It doesn't run by here," the man said.

He showed no sign of recognition. Smiling, he pointed down the hill. "Mill Pond Road, that's the nearest stop," he said in his smooth baritone. "In front of the shopping center."

"Thank you."

"My pleasure."

The man moved off, then started jogging as he turned in the lane leading to the barn-red house. He disappeared inside and all the lights went on. By then darkness had fallen, and when Dave looked down on the Ferguson acreage again, he could see nothing but the dim outline of the chimneys against a few faint stars, the sheen of water, and a few lighted windows. Diana's "ghost" had disappeared.

He hastened down the hill.

As he walked all perspective vanished. The trees rose and Red Mill Lane was just another long steep wooded road again. Philip Ferguson's ten-acre estate was totally hidden behind its border of trees and underbrush.

Dave paused before the gateposts.

As though from a great distance he could hear faint music. It floated through the trees. Somebody was playing the piano. As he stepped inside the driveway and started in under the trees, he recognized the tune. "Tales from the Vienna Woods."

Dave's mother had been a dancer, and had come from a little town in the Austrian Alps. She had loved this piece—and for a moment he paused, overwhelmed by a poignant memory which had nothing to do with Diana Roberts or this strange house and his fantastic situation. He was a kid of sixteen, running up the stairs with his schoolbooks, and "Tales from the Vienna Woods" was playing on the phonograph in the parlor where the French clock was. His mother was in the kitchen ironing. "Where's Poppa?" he had asked. "Oh, Poppa's not home yet from the show," she had replied airily. Dave's father had played fiddle in a movie house orchestra. But that was the day he had collapsed in the middle of a vaudeville act, and they had brought him up the stairs while "Tales from the Vienna Woods" was still playing on the phonograph.

Dave reached the open lawn.

The lights of the great house danced on the dark waters of the pond. The piano was still playing, and through the open windows he could see a crystal chandelier, a lamplit room, a vase of pink carnations and a woman's back, long black hair flowing down it. She was bent over a grand piano, playing. The music danced, cascaded, as her white fingers in long flowing sleeves of lavender flew back and forth over the keys. Then suddenly she stopped playing in the middle of the waltz, and put her dark head down into her hands. She sat alone, in the splendid bright room with all the lamps lit and the pink carnations trembling in a crystal vase on top of the piano.

A phone began to ring. But she sat there with her hands held over her face.

In the library, at the far left, a light went on.

A man was standing at a desk not far from the crimson curtains. He was speaking over the phone. He was small, middle-aged, and shrunken, with a freckled bald head and a face like a snapping turtle's. As Dave moved toward the library window, he stopped speaking and frowned. Then he laid the phone down.

"Cookie!" he called. "Cookie!"

"Yes." Dave heard a voice reply—from right behind him. "Yes, what is it, Uncle Alexander?" she called.

Then she gasped. He turned and faced her.

She was the blond girl he had seen near the pine trees.

She was about sixteen years of age. Her hair was long and straight and blond. She wore a white dress. On her teeth were braces. Close up, lit by the light streaming from the library window, she bore an unfortunate resemblance to the hawklike face of Philip Ferguson.

"Who are you? What are you doing?" she stammered, raising her hand to her mouth and drawing back.

Then she ran, screaming. "Uncle Alexander! Uncle Alexander!" By then Dave was racing for the driveway, the dark pines.

Eleven

The jukebox in Manny's delicatessen was going at full blast. Manny, the proprietor, was a great admirer of Elvis Presley. Dave sat in one of the back booths, sipping coffee and watching Mr. Kahn drink tea and consume a late meal. Through the long narrow store with its tiled floor and lindcruster walls the voice of Elvis belting out "Hound Dog" was almost completely blanketing conversation.

"That Philip Ferguson!" Mr. Kahn was saying amidst the din. "He was like a rotten apple in a barrel. He spoiled everything he came in contact with. Even his brother and his little daughter."

"Who?"

Mr. Kahn had spent the day at the New York Public Library reading old society and fashion magazines, carefully combing them for gossip items on the Ferguson clan.

"I haven't told you about his younger daughter?" Mr. Kahn popped a piece of rye bread thick with chicken liver into his mouth. "That poor kid. She has plenty good reason to hate him."

"What's her name?"

"Carol. They call her Cookie," Mr. Kahn replied. "She never even lived with her father. He hadn't had her to that house in years." He toyed with his saucer of coleslaw. "And what her father did to her mother, that makes it even worse."

"What did he do to her mother?"

"It's disgusting. He deserved everything that was coming to him."

"What did he do?"

"To Portia? Wait a minute and I'll tell you."

Mr. Kahn, lacking any clue to Diana's identity, had been drawing up a list of "suspects," people in Philip Ferguson's life who might have had powerful reasons to hate him. "Whether they killed him and framed you, that's a different story," Mr. Kahn said. By now, however, he had a list of about four people on whom he was doing very careful, intensive research.

Pushing his empty plate aside, he got out the black notebook, and as Elvis concluded "Hound Dog," and began on "Jailhouse Rock," he wet his forefinger and riffled through the closely written pages.

"Let me see. Oh, yes. Portia Ferguson. She was Philip Ferguson's *second* wife, you know. He married her in 1957." He looked over his spectacles at Dave, then down again to the notebook. "As I said, the daughter's name is Carol, or Cookie. Cookie is sixteen."

Dave kept thinking of that girl in the dusk with her braces and melancholy ugliness.

"You don't think *Cookie* was Diana?" he asked cautiously. "Diana was in her twenties."

"Wait a minute. Let me go on."

Holding the notebook toward the glaring ceiling light, he cleared his throat and read, "Portia Ferguson. Second wife. A blonde. Very talented actress and dancer at one time. Was twenty-five when Ferguson saw her. Had just achieved her first starring role in Broadway musical—after years of struggle and much help from her agent, Hyman Schneider, to whom she was engaged."

He picked up his tea and sipped it.

"Now listen to this," he said, after laying his cup down. "Philip Ferguson, then thirty-seven, divorced from his first wife, a society girl now dead, refused to take no for an answer. Courted the beautiful Portia with roses, champagne and sables. She succumbed. Married her in Detroit, Michigan. Honeymooned in Paris and Tanganyika. Brought her back to Red Mill Lane, and then proceeded to ignore her. Child, Carol, born in October 1958. Very shortly thereafter, Ferguson took Portia sailing. The seas were rough and she fell, badly injuring her back. In fact, the injury so bad she was crippled for life, confined to a wheelchair. A year after the injury Ferguson divorced her, leaving her and their baby girl in the care of her mother and a young blond sister in New York."

Mr. Kahn beamed.

"So—how's that for a suspect?"

"You mean Portia, from a wheelchair, and Carol, aged sixteen, arranged to murder Ferguson?" Dave asked. "The blond sister impersonated Diana?"

"It's possible. Or they might have hired someone. And Mr. Schneider, the agent, he could have done the actual shooting . . ." His voice trailed off. He twirled a rye bread crumb lying on the black formica table.

"It sounds a little far-fetched," Dave said.

"The best murders are far-fetched."

Elvis' strenuous voice rang through the delicatessen.

"Who else?" Dave asked at last. "You said something about his brother. Alexander. Isn't that his name?"

Small, balding, with a face reminiscent of a turtle's, Alexander Ferguson, now aged sixty-one, had spent his life in the shadow of his younger brother Philip. Taller, far stronger, and born with some mysterious charisma, the younger son had been his mother's darling, the family black sheep, but at the same time his father's secret favorite. Homer had scolded the boy but indulged him. He had laughed at his wild pranks, and threatened or paid off the people who would have punished him. Philip had ended up inheriting the family mansion on Red Mill Lane, most of the antiques and family heirlooms and half the family business—a business in which he had never taken the slightest interest, and in fact scorned. Whereas Alexander, who had no wife, no children and no sex appeal and who had worked sixteen hours a day in the family's textile empire, received exactly the same share—giving him no real control of the company unless his brother died.

"So as you can imagine, he's very happy about the present state of affairs," said Mr. Kahn, "since all he's lived for has been money. Aside, of course, from one thing."

"And what's that?"

"Snakes."

"*Snakes?*"

"He's an authority on huge reptiles—of the constrictor

variety. He has a basement full of them," said Mr. Kahn. "He likes to pet them and stroke them. And he has a whole menagerie of mice and rabbits he feeds them—after dinner every night."

Mr. Kahn ordered lemon meringue pie. "Blue Suede Shoes" jangled from the jukebox. Toying with his meringue, Mr. Kahn said across the table, "But the person I most suspect, Dave, the man I think had the biggest reason to kill him is a man named William Glaxton. He's already tried to once, and almost succeeded."

"Who's Glaxton?"

"A simple fellow. A garage mechanic."

"You haven't mentioned him before."

"I only heard about him yesterday—from that nice young girl from Toronto, Trench's secretary. I met her in the shopping center. We fell to chatting. I treated her to an ice-cream soda."

"Who did you tell her you were?"

"A friend of Isaac Bashevis Singer's. She admires his stories a great deal."

Dave laughed. "Okay—well, what about him?"

"It's a very long sad story."

Tackling his pie, Mr. Kahn began. It was indeed a very sad story, another horror tale in the life of Philip Ferguson.

Once William Glaxton had been a strapping handsome young man, an auto mechanic, with a beautiful blond wife, Helen. He adored her and was extremely jealous of her. Her figure was voluptuous, her hair ash-blond and childishly disheveled, and her smile angelic. People stared at her wherever she went.

But she seemed content with Glaxton. She seemed quite happy to keep house for him and wait for him to come home to the little frame bungalow in Norwalk. Every noon he hurried home to eat a hot lunch and go to bed with her, and in the afternoons she would sometimes saunter over to the garage to wait for him to get through work. Then he would wash up and take her out to dinner and a movie.

On one of these afternoons Philip Ferguson saw her.

He was thirty-three years old, still married, and he was driving a white Bentley. He wore a navy-blue blazer, and his hair, sun-bleached after a summer of sailing off Edgartown, was tousled above his deeply tanned and avid face. His two good bright blue eyes were bold—and instantly devouring.

Glaxton missed the interchange. He was sweating underneath a car. But three days later he came home at lunchtime to find Helen gone and a note scotch-taped to the icebox. Ferguson had picked her up in the Bentley. He and she were setting off across country, living the luxurious life she had read about in movie magazines, traveling from rich hotel to plush exclusive resort. Ferguson was buying her clothes, furs, jewelry. She was admired everywhere she went, and she adored admiration.

Glaxton stayed drunk for a month. He finally gave up trying to find her.

Ferguson abandoned the Bentley in San Francisco. He and Helen planed to Hawaii. There he abandoned Helen.

She was stupid, uneducated. She was beginning to bore him.

With all her fine clothes heaped around her in the beautiful hotel room looking out over the Pacific, she wrote a pitiful note to Glaxton, gave it to a bellboy to mail, and crawled nude into the king-size bed. There she swallowed twenty sleeping pills.

Back home in Norwalk Glaxton sold the bungalow and spent the proceeds on a marble tombstone with a marble angel on top. Then he went looking for Philip Ferguson.

He finally found him in the bar of the Stamford Yacht Club. Ferguson had just come in from a race that he had won in his boat, *The Rampage*, and was treating his crew to martinis served in a silver punch bowl. When Glaxton walked in, Ferguson bolted, but Glaxton caught him and knocked him to the floor. There Glaxton began stamping on him.

". . . and if the other men hadn't been there, he would have killed him," Mr. Kahn said. "As it was, Glaxton kicked out his eye. Ferguson was blinded in the process. That's how he came to lose it."

"God!" Dave said. "So what happened to Glaxton?"

"Oh, they put him in jail. Ferguson sued. And he collected damages."

"You mean the court made that poor guy pay *money* to that bastard?"

"Sure. It's no crime to commit adultery and abandon some poor girl so she commits suicide. But assault, the loss of one eye, that's a different proposition." Mr. Kahn wiped his lips with a paper napkin. "Excellent meringue."

"So you think Glaxton shot him?"

"Maybe. He's out of jail now. He was in Connecticut the night of the murder."

"Time's up, gentleman," said Manny. The delicatessen was closing. It was past eleven o'clock.

Dave walked Mr. Kahn back to his furnished room; then he walked slowly home through the deserted streets of Brooklyn. His head was spinning with sad tales and sad conjectures. Portia Ferguson and her sixteen-year-old daughter Cookie, Alexander Ferguson and his menagerie of snakes, and big blundering William Glaxton elbowing his way into the Stamford Yacht Club—all floated through his mind. But he could not concentrate on them long. He could concentrate only on Diana.

It was she and only she he really wanted to know about—who she was and why she had never called him since that night. It had been a week now, more than a week since she had touched him with her icy fingers and flitted down that driveway. He wondered if she was dead. He could not condemn her utterly. He knew that all the research in the world and all the facts Mr. Kahn might scribble down in his notebook could not compare with one word from her, one glimpse of her in her boots and her long black coat.

Diana was the key to everything.

In the apartment Momma was sitting up, waiting for him in her pink chenille bathrobe and hair net—like Patience on a monument.

"Any calls?" he asked.

"No calls." She rose to her feet anxiously. "You okay, Dave?" She pierced him with her x-ray eyes.

"Just fine."

"So what was keeping you so late?"

"Just playing chess," he said.

He closed the bedroom door.

On Friday afternoon he was in his classroom teaching. He had just confiscated two switchblades and was writing about the Jamestown colony on the blackboard when a monitor stuck her head in the door. "You're wanted in the principal's office, Mr. Marks. A phone call."

He didn't hurry. He was always getting phone calls—from social workers, policemen, and occasionally a parent. But the voice belonged to none of this ilk. It was soft and crystal clear, delightfully breathless and refined. "David? Is this David Marks? Hello, David." It chimed in the huge drab office like the voice of a delicate French clock. "I'm sick, David darling. I'm in the hospital . . . an emergency."

Then she hung up.

Twelve

An airport bus had just arrived and the sidewalk in front of the East Side Airlines Terminal was crowded with people. Then he saw a hand waving, and she darted out to the curb, with her blond hair flying and her eyes alight. She wore the long black coat, the boots.

"David. Thank God, David!" She grabbed the door handle and got in. "I was so afraid you wouldn't come."

"Where to?"

"I'm sorry, David."

"To Stamford?" he asked bitterly.

"Please, David. Don't," she faltered. "Just drive—anywhere you please."

He headed up Thirty-seventh Street through the warm sticky twilight. She lit a cigarette. "Okay, let's have it," he said. "Let's *have* it. What happened to you?"

"All *right.* I'm going to tell you." She was huddled in a corner, puffing nervously at the cigarette. "First I want you to know, David, that I just heard about it today. I've been out of the city for a week. I didn't know that any murder had been committed —until I read about it in the New York papers today."

"So—what happened to you a *week* ago?" he asked. "Why didn't you come back to the cab? Where've you *been* all this time, for God's sake?" Glowering, he turned his head toward her. "Why haven't you been in touch with me?"

"David, I'm sorry," she said in a low, contrite voice. "I just *couldn't* get in touch with you. My mother died—suddenly. I was at her sickbed . . . at her funeral . . . out west."

He kept silent. Then he said, "I'm sorry."

"Thank you," she said softly, humbly.

"Did you kill him, Diana?"

"*Me?* Did *I* kill him?" Her voice cracked. "David, I didn't even know that man was dead. I didn't know that there was anyone in that house. I swear to you, I didn't know that Mr. Ferguson—I'd never heard of him. And I had no idea of what had happened till I read about it in the papers today."

"Is that right?" David said.

"Yes. It is. I swear it," she replied.

He turned right on Madison Avenue. "So what were you doing in that house those three nights, may I ask?" he said. "What happened to you the night of the murder?"

"Nothing. I—I just left." Her voice was bell-like, clear. "I didn't see a single thing. I never went inside that house at all."

"Come *on*," he said.

"Never! I never went in there," she said vehemently, as he brought the cab to a halt on a street of handsome brownstones. "Not on *any* of those nights you took me. And on that last night I just ran."

"Where?"

"Through the trees and past the greenhouse and the tennis court, and out into the shopping center."

"How did you get home?"

"There was a bus. The last one. I caught it at the shopping center."

"A *bus!* You caught a *bus* from the shopping center!" For a long moment he stared at the pretty shadowy face, the anxious eyes. "My *God!*" he said softly, "and what about *me?* Didn't you ever think of me? I *waited* for you half an hour—and when you didn't come back, I *went* into that house!" His voice rose. "I looked all over for you."

"Oh, David. How very like you. I'm—sorry." She put her golden head into her hands.

"So what was the big idea—running off and leaving me like that?"

"I—couldn't help it." She did not look up. "I was ordered to," she said in a muffled voice.

"*Ordered* to? By whom?"

"The man who—who paid me—for the job." Lifting her head, she turned it uneasily toward the brownstones and the tree-shadowed sidewalk. "David, I—I'll explain everything—but please let's not stay here. Drive on."

"Why?"

"Because I'm frightened." Again she glanced around. "He warned me never to speak to you, never to go near you again. And—and he may not know I'm back in town. But I never can tell about—Dr. Corvo."

"Who?"

"Dr. Corvo. Wolfgang Corvo." She whispered the name.

Dave drove on, feeling elation and yet a nagging sense of disbelief. "Please don't lie to me, Diana," he said intensely. "I *went* into that house. I've been on the rack for over a week. Don't give me some cock-and-bull story."

"I'm not lying to you, David." From the shadows behind him, her voice was equally intense. "I'm going to tell you everything."

"Okay. Then *start*," he said.

"Except that when I'm finished explaining, you'll see that I don't understand a lot of it myself."

"Well—why don't you let me hear it?"

"You're *so* angry."

"I'm *not* angry."

"All right." She heaved a sigh. "I'll try to explain."

She lit a cigarette. A match flared, and mentholated smoke began to fill the cab. As he cruised slowly through the fashionable Murray Hill district, she began haltingly. "I—met this Dr. Corvo about a month ago—in New York. He said his first name was Wolfgang, and he seemed very nice and gentlemanly. He took me to wonderful places—like the theater and the ballet and gorgeous restaurants. And he never laid a hand on me. I was impressed—and rather flattered. He seemed a very intelligent and distinguished man. He's a scientist, a Ph.D."

"How old?"

"Middle-aged. Maybe in his forties. He has sandy hair that's turning gray."

In his rear-view mirror he could see her eyes looking anxiously into his own. When she saw him looking, she cast her eyes down, and then brushed vaguely at the smoke floating around her pale drawn face. She smiled wistfully.

"Go on."

"One night he drove me to this place in Connecticut, a restaurant that had a waterfall and swans. He asked me questions about my life and what I wanted most in the world. I said it was for my mother to get better, and finally he told me he had a proposition to make to me."

"Yes?"

"He drove me past some gateposts out in the country and said they led to the estate of a very, very wealthy man—a friend of his. He said that all he wanted me to do was take a cab up there on three different nights. He would pick the nights. I would get out of the cab and stay inside the grounds for just an hour, then take the same cab back again to New York."

Dave kept gripping the steering wheel, his jaw tightening.

"I was not to tell anybody about it," she went on. "I was not to tell the cabdriver a thing about what I was doing. I was to ask *him* not to tell anyone either, in fact, *insist* that he not tell anyone. And if I obeyed all the orders I would get into absolutely no trouble. The man who owned the house was away. The house was empty. I wouldn't even have to go inside it." She paused.

Dave grunted. "And you said yes—to all this junk?"

"Of course I did. You know I did. Who wouldn't have said yes—if they were poor and had to work hard for a living?"

"Where do you work?"

"In a sort of supper club, a fancy restaurant," she said hesitantly. "As a waitress. I couldn't make enough money modeling."

"What restaurant?"

"I'm not working there any more."

Dave drove down into the Park Avenue tunnel. It was fetid and smelled of urine on this warm April night.

"How much did Corvo pay you?" he asked her over his shoulder.

"Five thousand dollars," she replied.

The warm wind flew by.

"Plus the two hundred and forty I was given to pay *you*," she added. "At eighty dollars a ride."

"All in twenties?"

"All in twenties."

"And it never occurred to you that this wasn't exactly

kosher?" He came up again from the tunnel and crept along Park Avenue.

"Of course it did. But he kept telling me it was just a joke, a very private practical joke that he was playing on his wealthy friend."

"Yeah. Some joke. Some friend."

"And *I* couldn't see the harm in it," the pure young crystalline voice went on. "What could be so wrong, I asked myself, in just walking down through those beautiful pine trees and strolling around those lovely grounds for an hour? I enjoyed it. It was beautiful. I dipped my hand in that beautiful pond. I listened to the birds. I admired the daffodils and crocuses." She struck another match. "And I *loved* driving up there with you."

"What did you do the night it rained?"

"Oh." She hesitated. "I stayed in the greenhouse. It happened to be unlocked." She laughed. "And it smelled terrible. Of fertilizer."

"And the last night? Where did you stay?"

"I didn't. After I left you I just ran—through the grounds and out into the shopping center, as I've already told you."

"Dr. Corvo told you to do that?"

"Yes . . . that day," she said.

"But Corvo wasn't there that night?"

"I don't know. I didn't see him."

"Do you think Corvo shot him?"

"I don't *know,* David. I don't know *what* to think." Her voice was agitated, tremulous. "I only know I'm in a terrible mess. I was a fool . . . stupid . . . blind. I never should have said yes to him. I threw my whole life away—for nothing."

Her voice broke. She sounded close to tears. And later he would remember that moment and the quality of desolation in her voice. Every time he passed the Empire State Building or glimpsed the gilt towers of General Electric, he would recall her anguish, her despair.

"But I can't take it back now. It's done now. It's ruined me."

"Come on, Diana," he said. "Not necessarily. It isn't really that bad."

"It is," she said in a choked voice.

"Not if we help each other," he said. Then he took a deep breath. "What did this Dr. Corvo tell you about *me?*" he asked.

"You?" Her voice was faint.

"Yes. Didn't he tell you to pick me out especially?"

She hesitated. "Yes, in a way he did," she said.

"What did he tell you?"

"Well"—again she paused—"he said you were an excellent driver and he showed me a picture of you. He gave me your license number and told me to stand on a certain streetcorner and wait for you to come along. He said you were—outstandingly decent—a—a person I could trust and rely on—and he seemed to know all about you."

"Oh, my God!" Dave burst out. "Of course he did. Didn't you realize it was a setup?"

"A setup?"

"Against *me*. *I* was the one he planned to pin the murder on. *He'd* do the shooting. *I'd* take the rap for him. That's why he made you stay there for an hour—so I'd be seen for three nights by the neighbors," Dave said. "And that's why he made you run off—so *I'd* go in there. *I'd* be blamed. And I'd have absolutely no proof you'd ever been with me."

There was dead silence. "My God," she quavered finally. "Is—that true?"

"It's true as hell, Diana. *I'm* the one in trouble," he said. "For five thousand, two hundred and forty bucks, he got himself a perfect alibi. He really figured it."

"But—but I don't altogether understand."

"He hired you—to get me up there—so I'd be blamed for committing the crime."

"But how *could* you be blamed?" she cried. And in the rear-view mirror he could see her staring blankly at him. "What motive would you have, David? A murderer has to have a motive. A murderer has to know his victim. And *you* certainly didn't know that Mr. Ferguson—any more than *I* knew him. Why would you kill him when you didn't have a reason?"

He sat without speaking. Numbly he kept driving, up one Manhattan street and down another.

"You didn't, did you, David?"

His palms on the steering wheel were wet. Slowly, carefully, he wiped them over his knees.

"Or—or did you?"

"No," he answered slowly. "I didn't have any reason for

77

killing him." Then he turned his head. "But I'm driving us to Stamford, Diana. Right now. We're turning ourselves in to the police."

"We? Us?" she faltered.

He started west, crosstown. "David, wait," she said. "I'll have to think about it."

"No," he said. He kept on driving.

"It's much too overwhelming and confusing, all of it." She was leaning forward. "What you've told me—about yourself. It puts a totally different picture on things. It scares me. I'm afraid."

"Well—*don't* be. *We* didn't do anything."

"But I took his money. I've spent that money. It paid for my mother's operation—and her funeral expenses."

"So what?" Dave said.

"And they might call me an accomplice." Her voice shook. "David, please stop. And let me think about it overnight. Give me a day or two—and let me find out more."

"No."

They crossed Fifth Avenue, not far from the spot where Fran had been killed six months ago. "I'm afraid of him," she blurted out in a choked voice. "I'm afraid to tell on him—for what he might do to us both."

"Don't be. I'll protect you."

"But he's weird. He has weird connections. He's a very strange, peculiar man."

"That doesn't matter."

"I'm alone in the world. He could kill me. Or his people could. He knows everything about me, where to find me." She was gasping, squirming on the back seat now. "David, please—stop and let me out. I can't rush into it at a moment's notice. Slow *down* a minute." She rapped on the glass. "I'll call you. In a day or two."

"Unh-unh."

They were entering the theater district. They were stopped by a light on Seventh Avenue. Crowds surged across, and a policeman's whistle blew. Holding up an orange arm, whistle still shrilling in his mouth, the policeman advanced toward Dave, while armies of pedestrians, close-packed, surged across the intersection.

"Whatsa matter with you, Mac? Get back!" the policeman snarled. Then suddenly Dave heard the cab door open. And she was out and running, darting toward the curb and melting into the neon-lit crowds.

"Diana!"

"I'll call you!" she shouted and kept running. There were cars to left and right, a sea of people on either side. The policeman's whistle blew again, and horns honked behind him. But he jerked the steering wheel and somehow managed to turn the corner, stop and look over his shoulder for a few seconds.

He glimpsed her still running, zigzagging through the crowds surging beneath an enormous sign on which a vast lighted mouse was dancing, pirouetting. Then she disappeared for good into the sea of people.

"Corvo? Wolfgang Corvo?" Mr. Kahn said when Dave called him in Bensonhurst ten minutes later. "A scientist? A Ph.D.? Offhand I never heard of him, but I'll get to work on it."

"Thanks, Mr. Kahn."

"Meanwhile I'd do nothing."

"I wasn't planning to," Dave said.

"Good boy," said Mr. Kahn.

Thirteen

Dave woke that Saturday morning with a feeling of dread and doom. All night long he had dreamed of Diana—Diana with her hands strapped behind her, her eyes wide and her black boots beating a tattoo on a bare wooden floor. Her white breasts were exposed. A sandy, gray-haired man was flicking a knife across her throat. When he woke, he was in a sweat, and in the silent darkness of the apartment, he thought he heard the phone ringing. But when he got up, Momma still snored and the alarm clock ticked on the refrigerator.

Now it was morning, and Momma was standing in the doorway of his bedroom dressed in her black coat, white gloves and a pillbox hat with a veil.

"So I'm off to the funeral."

"What funeral?"

"Teresa McCarthy's. My old landlady," she said. "I told you she died two days ago. It's a Catholic funeral—at nine in the Bronx."

"Oh." He rubbed his head. "Well, have a good time."

"A good *time?* At a *funeral?*" From the doorway she frowned at him. "Dave, you're starting to worry me."

"I'm just tired." He stretched and yawned.

"Never mind. Something funny is going on—and we're going to talk about it the minute I get back!"

With this remark she departed, leaving him alone with the children. In the kitchen Joel was running around in his pajamas, and Jeremy, still strapped in his high chair, was beating with a wooden spoon on the tray.

"Daddy, will you take us to Coney Island?" Joel asked.

"Coney Island?" Dave sat down and started dialing Mr. Kahn's number.

"Grandma bought me a kite, Daddy. She said you'd teach me how to fly it—at Coney Island," Joel said.

Mr. Kahn's number did not answer.

The apartment smelled of cooking and stale bedding. Dishes were piled up in the sink. Last night he had looked for Wolfgang Corvo's number in every phone book for every borough. He had called directory assistance. Directory assistance didn't have him listed in New York or Connecticut—even for an unlisted number.

Dave sat drumming on the shaky end table beside the telephone.

"Want to see it?" Joel stood next to him.

"See what?"

"My kite." Joel brought it. It was red and enormous, nearly as big as Joel, who rattled it up and down the apartment, trying to make it fly above the chairs and tables. He knocked Fran's picture over. "Careful," Dave said. "Put it away now."

"*When* are we going, Daddy?"

"Where?"

"Coney Island."

"Later. Get some clothes on."

Mr. Kahn had undoubtedly left for the New York library or Stamford, Connecticut. With the New York phone book on his knees Dave sat down and started making a list of scientific research foundations in Manhattan. Suddenly there was a cry from Joel from the next room.

"Daddy, look!" He heard a blow and then a wail. "Dumdum!" Joel shrilled angrily. "Now we'll never go to Coney Island!"

In the middle of the bedroom floor stood Jeremy, with nothing but his training pants on, tears on his long lashes, panic in his eyes; he quickly dropped the purple crayon on the rug. Purple scribbles festooned the walls. Then he ran for cover under his crib.

"I sorry," he sobbed, his little rump sticking up in the air.

"Oh, my God. Jerry, what got into you?" Dave picked him up, feeling ashamed. He had neglected them, practically ignored them during the past two weeks—ever since Diana Roberts had

81

walked into his life. Since the morning after the murder he had been in a daze on the rare occasions when he'd been home, and had not taken them anywhere, not even to the local playground. But the sun was shining, it was Saturday, a beautiful day in spring, and he couldn't let them rot all day in this dreary, stuffy apartment.

"Okay, okay. Put some clothes on and we'll go out."

"To Coney Island?"

"Yes."

"Yippee!" Joel screamed and shouted for joy. They pulled clothes out of the bureau drawers and put them on backwards in their excitement. Joel even helped Jeremy tie his shoelaces, and after they were tied, ran up and down with the kite trailing, bumping along the floor behind him.

Jeremy hummed. And finally Dave spied him toddling into the bathroom, where he picked up a wet washcloth, returned to the bedroom and tried to erase his handiwork from the walls.

The phone rang.

"Don't answer it," Joel said tensely. Both boys were dressed and waiting for him. Jeremy was carrying a rusty pail and shovel.

"Hello."

"Is this the residence of David Marks?" Her voice was guarded. It sounded far away.

"Yes. Diana?"

"David, this is Diana."

"I know it's Diana." He sat down on the sofa. "What was *that* about last night?"

"I'm sorry. I *saw* him. He was right behind us—in another cab."

"Come on. Be honest."

"I *am* honest. David, I've got to see you again."

"When?"

"*Now*," she said. "Right now."

He glanced at the two children. Joel was fidgeting, scowling, watching him.

"I couldn't make it right now," he said.

"Why? It's *urgent!*"

"My mother-in-law's away, and I promised my kids I'd take

them to Coney Island. But if you'll give me your phone number—"

"Where in Coney Island?"

"The beach. The boardwalk. We're going to try to fly a kite."

"I'll look for you," she said.

"Diana—"

There was a click and then the dial tone.

High above the beach and the sparkling ocean soared the red kite. It dipped and swooped and pirouetted while Joel, his face a study in ecstasy, held tightly to the stick round which the string was wrapped.

"How high is it now, Daddy?"

"Oh—pretty high."

"A mile? Ten miles?"

Dave gazed up and down the cold, gray deserted beach. Nearby on the sand sat Jeremy with his shoes and socks off, wriggling his bare toes. He was smiling vaguely at the ocean and grabbing handfuls of sand in his fists. He was humming. They had been there for at least an hour and still she had not appeared.

"What makes it go, Daddy?"

"What?"

"The kite."

"Oh—the wind."

"What's the wind?"

Dave stood with his hand on his little son's shoulder, trying to forget Diana Roberts for at least a few minutes. The wind was invisible, he said. It was what Joel felt against his cheek and what was tousling Jeremy's brown curls. It was strong and immensely powerful. It circled the earth and came and went and brought the rain and dried the rain. Joel was barely listening. He was watching the red kite. To him it was pure magic, a thing with its own life, a strange wonderful bird he was possessed of and controlling high in the clouds.

Dave glanced again at his watch. It was one-fifteen.

A few people sauntered along the windy boardwalk. The surf rolled in with a thundering crash. From far away he could hear the sound of wheezy music and from the bleached white stands across the way smell the odor of popcorn and frankfurters.

"Daddy!"

From the sky the kite was falling, fluttering wildly out of control.

Dave grabbed the string and tried to haul it in. But the wind was too strong. The string snapped and off down the beach flew the kite, with Joel staggering after it. It fluttered out over the ocean, swooped down over the surf; finally a wave swallowed it.

"Daddy!"

Joel ran into the foaming water, up to his ankles in freezing surf, and then bent double with anguish.

"Come on. Don't cry." Dave patted him and tried to pick him up. "I'll buy you another one."

"I don't want another one."

"All right, but let's get out of this water before you catch cold. Dry your feet. Put your shoes on."

The boy refused to be comforted. As Dave rubbed the cold little ankles, Joel wept as though his heart would break. Joel had not shed a tear when Momma told him about Fran, nor had he once asked about his mother since her death. But now as though the loss of the kite had opened a deeper wound and released some hidden reservoir of sorrow, he sobbed without restraint, his head against Dave's chest.

"David . . . David Marks . . ."

From the boardwalk overhead, Diana Roberts was calling him.

Slender and starkly dramatic in the long black coat and boots, she was standing outlined against the sky, one hand resting on the wooden railing. She wore a black turban around her head. It totally concealed her hair and emphasized the sharpness of her cheekbones.

"David, I've looked everywhere for you."

Gingerly she descended the steps, holding the skirts of her coat. "Are these your children?" In the light of day she looked pale and washed-out-looking, and there were tiny golden freckles sprinkled across her nose.

"Yes," he said.

"What are their names?"

"Joel and Jeremy, this is Miss Roberts."

"Hi, Joel. Hi, Jeremy." Her eyes glowed for a moment. Smiling, she stooped down to their level. But the children stared at her solemnly. Joel surveyed her up and down.

"I *love* children. They're just darling." Her eyes were green, not blue. "David, I haven't got much time, actually."

"Okay, kids, run along and play."

Still staring at her, they made off.

"Adorable." She watched them wistfully. Then with a total change in tone and manner she moved closer to him across the sand. "David, I've made up my mind definitely. I think you *should* go to the police. We can't let Corvo get the better of us."

"Good. I'm glad to hear it," he said.

Her face looked plainer in the light of day—and younger. She was wearing no make-up except for the mascara, and her skin looked almost transparently white, like paper, in the brilliant sunlight. She looked unhealthy, like someone who had been indoors for weeks.

"He's a sadist, a very evil man," she was saying. "I've learned some new things about him—just today. And he *did* know Philip Ferguson. Do you know what he was doing? He was *blackmailing* him—all that time. He knew some awful secret about him."

"Is that so? Where did you hear this?"

"From a friend of mine. A person who knows him." She glanced up at the boardwalk and then began to walk away from the flight of sandy steps. "He also followed me for blocks last night before I managed to lose him . . . So he knows I've talked to you."

"You're actually in danger?"

"Am I!" She glanced up at the bright blue sky. She gave a bitter little laugh. "He warned me that if I *ever* told a soul about those trips to Stamford, he'd kill me."

"But you didn't say that last night."

"I know, but he really said it. And he meant it, I'm sure he did."

Circling the sands, she chafed her hands. Her head averted in the ugly black turban, her coat sweeping out behind the slender legs in boots and skimpy mini-skirt, she paced like some strange bird which had alighted on the wintry beach—totally ignoring the surf, the sun, the sky, and the two children watching her from the water's edge.

"Do you know where I'm living now?" she said. "In the subway. That's where I'm living. I checked out of my hotel last night."

"Diana—"

Thin and wind-blown, she shivered on the cold gray beach. Then she raised her eyes to him with a desperate pleading look. "So you have my permission, David . . . to *stop* him, do whatever you can."

"Okay." He took her arm. "Then let's get out of here. Why don't you just come home with me?"

"Come *home* with you?"

"Why not? It's a whole lot better than the subway."

She looked at him for a second, then a spasm flickered over her face. "David, oh, David," she choked, and shook her head.

"Come on," he said, and he drew her closer to him. "There's nobody there, and we can talk about it, have some tea."

"Oh, my God."

She leaned against him, trembling, half laughing and half crying, and he could see Joel staring at them from a distance, against the rolling, crashing surf.

"Oh, poor David. You're such a good person. What an insane world this is."

Tears coursed down her cheeks. The tears mingled with the mascara and the eye liner, streaking her pale face with black and making her eyes even more pathetic and sad.

"I couldn't possibly go home with you, David." Briefly she laid her head on his shoulder. He could feel her warm breath on his neck. "I'd love to, but I'm desperate. Can't you realize how desperate I am."

"Of course, and I'm crazy about you."

In spite of the turban and the runny make-up, he had never found her so appealing. He put his arm around her, tried to draw her close.

"I know you are. I know it." Her voice was broken. Her body was trembling.

"All I want is to take care of you."

"Then—go to the police, David!"

With a sweeping gesture she broke loose from him, and throwing her arms wide, looked wildly toward the clouds, the dazzling sun.

The surf pounded. The wind blew.

"Well—sure," he said. "We'll go together."

"Together."

Her head drooped, her arms sagged slowly to her sides. And she stood motionless in the black turban, the black coat.

"There's nothing to be afraid of," he said, advancing to her. "I don't know how many times I have to tell you that. As long as we're together—as long as we *both* confirm each other's stories— then we have nothing to fear." He laid his hand on her frail shoulder. "*You* know all about Dr. Corvo and where to find him—and I know all about these cab rides back and forth."

"I don't know where to find him," she said in a stifled voice.

"Then how do you get in touch with him?"

"I don't. He gets in touch with *me*."

"Okay, it doesn't matter." Her body was still rigid. "We don't even have to wait to go to Stamford," Dave said. "We can walk into any police station—right here in Coney Island."

"Yes?" Her head still drooped.

"Any officer can take our deposition."

"Is that right?"

"Of course, Diana . . . They'll be so happy to hear the truth, they've been looking so long for *any* suspect—they'll fall on our necks, I'm sure."

She turned—at last.

"O–kay, David."

Her eyes were green and blank. Her face was white and drawn.

"I'll go with you," she whispered. "I'll try not to be frightened."

"Good. Thank God," he said. And he kissed her hard on her ice-cold lips. He held her tight and heard her cry as she relaxed for just an instant against him.

"Call the children, and let's go." He felt her hot tears on his cheek.

With a full heart he turned and called them. They were chasing each other along the curling edges of the ocean, their small bodies backlighted by the sun.

"Joel! Jeremy!"

Giggling, they kept running in and out of the glistening shallows over the wet sand. He shook his head and grinned. He took a few steps toward the water and raised his voice.

"Hey, Joel. Hey, Jeremy. Come here." He turned back to her, smiling. "They're usually much better behaved," he began. But even as he spoke, his voice died in his throat.

She was already at the top of the boardwalk steps, sand flying from the heels of her boots, her coat swirling out behind her.

"Diana!"

"I can't, David. I've changed my mind. I'm sorry." Thinly, breathlessly she called back to him over her shoulder as she ran. "I'll be in touch," she cried. He heard the terror in her voice. He heard the tattoo of her boots on the hollow wooden boardwalk.

"Diana. Stop. *Diana!*"

She ran on, a dwindling stick figure in the sun.

He bought the children lunch at a concession. From a boardwalk phone booth he called Mr. Kahn. Mr. Kahn's number still did not answer. Outside the merry-go-round he tried again. But the Bensonhurst number rang and rang, and even the dentist who sometimes picked up the phone after ten or eleven rings did not answer this afternoon. By then it was two-thirty, and at three o'clock he started for home, dreading to leave the beach somehow, feeling that he would never see its blue serenity, its golden peace again.

Down the long boardwalk they trudged. He carried Jeremy in his arms. On the subway Joel kept asking him questions about the wind. The child was still chattering eagerly when they came slowly up the block, and Dave saw the police car parked in front of the apartment entrance.

He stopped short. He stood still.

"What's the matter, Daddy?" Joel tugged at his trouser leg.

"Nothing."

Shifting the sleeping Jeremy in his arms, Dave took a deep harsh breath. Then he walked on into the apartment lobby.

Fourteen

As he turned the key, he could hear Momma talking excitedly. A man's deep voice answered. Everything had been pointing to this moment. Mr. Kahn to the contrary, it had been inevitable. He opened the door and walked in.

"Dave!"

Momma's face was pale and anxious. She had come into the foyer. Still wearing the black dress she had worn to Mrs. McCarthy's funeral, she ignored the children and turned back to the living room. "Dave, these two gentlemen want to see you. They're from the police."

A big gray-haired man advanced. "David Marks?"

"Yes, I am."

"Yes, this is my son-in-law," Momma said in a strained voice.

"Lieutenant Romano," the man said. He was swarthy, dressed in a tan raincoat. "And Officer Crandall." On the sofa sat a black man dressed in uniform. "We're from Homicide."

Dave nodded. "Yes?"

Jeremy had awakened. He was stirring, squirming in Dave's arms. Dave set him down and the child swayed groggily, blinking, whimpering a little. But Momma made no move to help. Dave picked him up again. "Will you excuse me for a minute?" he said. "Come on, Joel."

Joel's eyes were round with curiosity. He was standing, staring at Crandall.

"I'll take care of them," said Momma, shooing Joel away from the sofa. As she took Jeremy from Dave's arms, she again looked questioningly into Dave's eyes. Seldom had he seen her more distraught. The bedroom door closed, and he heard Joel say, "Grandma, is that a real policeman?" "Shh!" she replied. Then there was total silence from the small cramped rooms beyond.

Romano smiled. "Cute kids."

"Thank you."

"How old?"

"Six and two," Dave said.

"And your mother-in-law takes care of them? You never remarried?" Romano asked. "This is the family—just the four of you, living here?"

"Yes."

Dave's eyes remained fixed on the match Romano was striking and on the curl of smoke rising from his thin brown cigar.

"Okay, I'll come to the point, Mr. Marks. Your wife was killed on the night of October 16 last year by a hit-and-run driver, is that right?" Romano sat down. "In Manhattan at the corner of Fifty-first and Fifth, around two o'clock in the morning?"

"Yes." Dave's fist tightened, relaxed.

From his raincoat pocket Romano drew a slip of paper. He took out a pair of half-glasses and looked over them with brown bloodshot eyes. "You reported that the car was a small black foreign convertible and the driver was a middle-aged man with gray hair. He wore a patch over his left eye. Is that correct?"

"Right," Dave replied.

"But you weren't able to make note of the license-plate numbers or even be sure of the color of the plates?"

"No, I wasn't able to."

"You did say you could identify the man—if you ever saw him again."

"Yes."

Romano again smiled—faintly. "You even set out to look for him yourself, is that right?"

Dave nodded. He sat down, resting his elbow on the television set. On top of it was Fran's picture, the lovely delicate sweet face with the soft brown hair pulled back and curling about the temples. She smiled at him, eternally wistful, from her silver frame. Romano's gaze followed his own.

"I don't blame you. Beautiful girl. Your wife?"

Dave nodded. "Thanks."

His arm felt stiff. Every muscle felt rigid. And perspiration was beginning to spring from his armpits and trickle down his sides. Romano rose and brandished his cigar.

"Well, we've got some news for you," Romano said. "We think we've found the car—the black convertible."

Dave stared. His throat constricted.

"We think we've even found the driver," Romano said.

"Who?"

"A man named Philip Ferguson."

Dave kept gripping the polished edge of the old TV set.

"A resident of Stamford, Connecticut," Romano said—with a geniality in his tone that Dave found puzzling. "The car was an MG. A brand-new MG convertible. Black, with a black top. He'd just brought it over from England."

Dave moved his hand from the TV set and rested it on his knee. He was aware that Officer Crandall was watching him silently, impassively, from the yellow sofa.

"Where was it found?" he finally forced out.

"In an old unused quarry," Romano said. "Deep in the woods, lying in a puddle, behind some rocks overgrown with weeds. It had evidently been driven in there some time ago. The paint was rusted, the top had rotted, and one license plate had been hacked off—but the car was definitely Ferguson's. He lived only half a mile away."

"I—see."

Romano smiled faintly, his eyes fixed steadily on Dave. "Ferguson also happened to have one eye. Over the left one he wore an eye patch."

Dave blinked. He swallowed. "He's—confessed?" he asked.

"Ferguson is dead."

For the first time Officer Crandall spoke, and his voice was deep, in the bottom of his chest. "He was murdered two weeks ago."

"Two weeks ago." Dave's voice was a dull echo.

"Yeah," Romano said.

"Shot in the back with a .22-caliber bullet," rumbled Crandall. Then they both stared at him steadily across the small, untidy living room, and from the closed door of the bedroom he could hear the sound of Momma's breathing.

He got up slowly. He walked to the window. On the street

below he could see the police car, still parked in front of the apartment entrance. He thought of Diana—and her terror last night and this afternoon when he had begged her to go to the police with him. He thought of Mr. Kahn, rocking in a bay window in Bensonhurst and telling him to hold out until the last possible minute.

"I still don't get it," he said. Taking a deep breath, he turned back to the two policemen. "If this Ferguson is dead, then how do they *know* he killed my wife?"

"The car was damaged," Crandall replied. "The radiator was dented. It had been missing since the night of the accident, October 16."

"Did Ferguson's wife report it missing?" Dave asked.

"No, she didn't know about the accident," Romano said. "She was away the night it happened, visiting her family in Cicero, Illinois." He puffed on his cigar.

"Then how do they know it killed my wife?"

"An anonymous tipster," Officer Crandall said.

"Anonymous?"

"Somebody called the Stamford police and said Ferguson had told them he'd been in a fatal accident on October 16 last year and had dumped the car in the quarry," Romano said. "They said the car was still there."

"You don't know the name of this person?"

"Unh-unh," Romano shrugged. "They refused to give their name. But they felt the facts shouldn't be kept a secret any longer."

"Was it a man or a woman?"

"I have no idea," Romano said. "The report just said anonymous."

"I see."

Dave looked from one face to another. He felt his head beginning to pound.

Romano smiled at him blandly. "*You* didn't happen to know about that car? Nobody *called* you and told *you* it was in the quarry?"

Dave stared back at him. "No, of course not," he said emphatically.

"Ever hear of Philip Ferguson?" Still genially, Romano waved his cigar.

"No."

"Or ever looked for him in Stamford?"

"Never."

His nerves were pounding in his brain like hammers on an anvil.

"Ever see this man before?"

Romano thrust the picture under Dave's nose. It was a small glossy photograph, the same likeness of Philip Ferguson Dave had seen in the newspapers. "Was this the man you saw in the MG, the driver of the car that killed your wife?"

Dave gazed at the hawklike face with its thatch of thick gray hair. He tried to keep his expression impersonal. "Yes," he said at last. "Yes, I think it is—yes." He closed his eyes. "Yes, that's the man I saw while I was lying there on the sidewalk. He stopped the car for just a second, slammed on the brakes—and then he sped off, leaving my wife lying in the gutter with her back broken and her face—pulp."

He broke off. He handed the picture back to Romano.

"We understand," said Officer Crandall in his rumbling preacher's voice.

And then Romano was ambling toward the door. "Okay. I guess that just about does it." He turned to Crandall, who was still sitting on the sofa. "Joe?"

Crandall got up, unfolding his long lean body slowly. He gazed around the room, fingering his policeman's cap. Finally his eyes returned to Dave.

"We have your occupation listed as schoolteacher, Mr. Marks." Looking solemnly into Dave's eyes, he asked, "Are you *still* a schoolteacher?"

"Yes, I am."

A moment longer Crandall looked deep into his eyes. Then he moved to the doorway, and pausing there, said gravely, "Good night and thank you, Mr. Marks."

"Good night."

The elevator door closed over them.

Listening to the wind roar up the elevator shaft, he shut the door, locked it, put the chain-bolt on, and then moved to the telephone.

"Dave!"

She came toward him in her black dress as he held the

receiver in his hands. Her face was chalk-white, her eyes tear-filled. "Dave, it's true? He's dead? They found him?"

"Yes, Momma."

He turned and faced her—feeling deep sorrow.

"His name was Ferguson? A man up in Connecticut?"

"Yes, Momma."

She was trembling violently. He pressed her hand. He put his arms around her and patted her. "Be glad he's dead, Momma. Punished. Somebody killed him."

"Yes, Dave." She looked up into his face strangely. "That still doesn't bring her back, Dave." In hoarse tones she said, "Nothing could bring her back—my beautiful daughter!" Again she searched his face with a curious fearful look. "Never did I want him found, Dave. Never did I pray that you would find him. I prayed that you would never find him—your whole life!"

"And I didn't, Momma. Someone else did."

"Ach!"

She drew in her breath sharply. Turning her back on him, she stared out the window through the white curtains at the gathering dusk. Then she turned. "You're telling me you didn't kill him?"

"Of *course* not."

"Please." She fingered a ruffle. "Don't kid me, son. Don't lie to me."

"Momma!"

She walked from him heavily, blindly, past the chairs, the lamps, the TV set. "For two weeks now you've been keeping something from me. You've been thinking I didn't notice. But I knew—something was wrong."

"Momma, listen to me. I didn't do it."

"Not eating. Not paying attention. Coming home every night so late," she moaned. "And every time the phone rings, you jump. And Kahn, he's always sneaking around. You're whispering together."

"Momma, *I didn't kill him!*"

"Not that I'd blame you. You loved her. He deserved it."

She was sobbing. He took her hand. "Momma, look. I didn't kill him. I didn't even know he was the driver, and I've got a million things to worry about, new developments I've got to discuss with Mr. Kahn."

"Why Kahn? What's Kahn got to do with it?"

Dave shrugged. He picked up the phone. "Once I talk to him, I'll tell you everything—but it's urgent now, Momma. And I need his advice." He began to dial. "It's very complicated."

"What kind of advice? If you didn't kill him, what's so complicated?"

Mr. Kahn's number rang twice and then the phone was picked up and a male voice said hello.

"May I speak to Mr. Kahn, please?" Dave asked.

"He's not here. He's in the hospital," the man replied. Dave recognized him as the dentist who owned the house in Bensonhurst.

"The hospital?" He felt cold all over.

"Yes, he had a heart attack this afternoon," the dentist said. "He was taken ill on the subway coming back from Connecticut."

Fifteen

Mr. Kahn was in the intensive care unit and they could see him for only a few minutes. He lay looking very small and shrunken in the high hospital bed. Momma and Dave stood beside him, watching his chest flutter up and down and the needle quivering back and forth on the dial behind his bed. His paper-thin bluish eyelids flicked open for just a moment and flicked closed. Then it was time to go.

"Kahn is tough," Momma said as they walked down the hospital corridor. "He'll get better. He won't die." She repeated it like some forlorn refrain as she twisted her wedding ring.

"Why don't you marry him, Momma?"

"Maybe I will—if he gets better—and *you* get straight. He's asked me often enough," she said.

They sat in the living room. The boys were in bed, asleep. "So now what, Dave? What's going to happen to you—without Kahn?"

"Nothing. I'll be okay."

But it was as though he had lost an arm or a leg or a brain. And he felt terribly guilty. The old man had overtaxed himself beyond all reason on his behalf—running back and forth to the library, covering half the state of Connecticut, in his frantic efforts to come up with a solution—and Dave knew he should have stopped him. He should not have permitted him to embark on the project at all.

Momma rose from the sofa. By now he had told her everything. Pushing the newspapers he had showed her aside, she walked to the window and back. "You want my advice, Dave, I say go to the police. Forget about that blond *shiksa* and her Dr. Corvo. Forget about Kahn." She pointed a finger at him. "Go to the police. Tell them what you know. Tell the police the truth. All of it. Right now."

"No, Momma." He shook his head.

"Why not, for God's sake?"

"I still have some time left."

"*Time?*" She tossed her head. "With the police here today already? Asking you every question in the book?"

"They still haven't made the main connection," he said. "They still think I'm just a schoolteacher."

"So?"

"According to the police, a *cabdriver* shot Ferguson. But a *schoolteacher's* wife was killed."

"Oh." She thought about it for a minute, then shrugged and walked away. "They'll find out about you soon enough," she said. She turned, looking sharply at him. "You still think that *shiksa's* gonna help you, I suppose?"

Dave was silent.

"She's *never* gonna help you," Momma said emphatically. "Three times she took you up there—and two weeks it took her to call you up after she ran off on that bus."

"I know, Momma. I know."

"And twice," she bristled at the walls, "she tells you to go to the police without her, but *she* won't go with you herself. She runs off like a rabbit. That's some fine person, I assure you."

"Look, Momma."

"That's some fine girl friend of yours."

"She isn't any girl friend," he said, reddening and walking from her toward his bedroom. "But she's my only alibi. And she's got to be willing to testify—that she hired me to take her up there, and a guy named Dr. Corvo hired *her* so I could take the rap for him. It's a worthless story, Momma; it will just sound crazy to the police unless she's willing to confirm it."

"And what makes you think she's gonna confirm it?"

"Because I think she really wants to."

"Hah! So why isn't she calling you then?"

He ran his hand through his hair. "She's scared. She's scared to death, Momma. That guy Corvo has done a real job on her."

Then he left the living room. He left the apartment. He paced the streets like a caged animal.

Time was crowding him to the wall. Yet his instinct was still not to run to the police, to panic. If he could not altogether trust Diana Roberts, he still had to trust Mr. Joseph Kahn, who had emphasized the importance of patience, and stoicism and silence. Although Mr. Kahn lay gasping for breath behind the walls of a city hospital, he was still the smartest man Dave knew, and even now Dave could hear his voice from the bow-window as the rocker creaked and the petals fell from the flowering tree.

"Wait," the old man had said. "Any moment can produce a miracle." And "If one waits and does nothing, then the murderer will have to take the lead. It will be *he* who has to make the moves—and in doing so, he may give himself away." And "Wear him down with patience—silence. Remember that he's only human. He can crack under pressure, and lose the game."

Up and down the streets of Brooklyn Dave walked—trying not to notice cop cars or cringe at the sound of sirens . . .

In the newspapers the next day he read about the finding of the car in the quarry. Most of the items were brief, but in one paper called the *Daily Witness*, a sensational tabloid which specialized exclusively in scandal, there was a long article on the subject and a picture of Mrs. Ferguson watching the car being hauled out of the quarry. Her back to the camera, her dark hair hanging down over her short belted raincoat, she was flanked by two state troopers.

SHARON SHOCKED. KNEW NOTHING, the headlines said.

On an inside page there was a small cameo likeness of Fran with her wistful smile, and in a boldface box headed VOWS VENGEANCE, Dave himself was quoted as having said, "It was a black foreign convertible. A man with a black eye patch was driving it. I'll never forget that face. I'll kill him if I ever find him." There was no picture of Dave, but the article said he had identified Ferguson as the driver of the car.

Sharon Ferguson had been interviewed by a female reporter from the *Witness* in her home on Red Mill Lane. She was "shocked and overwhelmed" by the news, she told the reporter. She had not been home the weekend of the accident. On the night of October 16 she had been away, she told police, visiting her sick mother in Cicero, Illinois. "It was the first time I had ever left my husband since our marriage," she said. On her return home from the Middle West, he had not told her about the accident, she said. "In fact, he seemed rather cheerful, and had bought me a diamond bracelet."

When he met her plane at Kennedy, she said, he had not been driving the MG. "I remember we drove back in our white Ford station wagon. But I didn't think anything of it at the time. We own four cars and were always interchanging them. The MG was *his* car, really, something *he* liked to drive."

As the days and weeks passed, she said, she had not really noticed the MG's absence either. "I suppose I just assumed," she said, "that the horrid little thing was in the repair shop where Phil was always sending it to have it worked on. He had bought it in England in August, but he could never buy a car without having its engine overhauled—revved up to go a great deal faster. Or adding new gadgets like stereo tapes and special cigarette lighters. I remember he called this car his 'Fun Car for 1973'—but I seldom drove it. I hated it. It was so tiny, with poor visibility, and a thorough nuisance to drive."

She wanted the family, the "husband of that poor young girl who was killed" to know that they had her sympathy. She was sure her own husband had been "tortured by incessant guilt" ever since the accident had occurred—and that the back trouble he had suffered from for the past six months had been a psychosomatic symptom of that guilt. "And I wish I could say," she had stated to the *Daily Witness* reporter, "that it wasn't Phil's MG or Phil wasn't driving it that night—but since that young man in Brooklyn, that schoolteacher, *saw* Phil in the car and says that it was he, then there is nothing more that I can say except I'm sorry."

None of the neighbors on Red Mill Lane had known anything about the car in the quarry either. All expressed shock and pity for Mrs. Ferguson and the young victim of the accident, but none knew or could even guess the identity of the "anonymous tipster," who had phoned the news in to the police.

"I find this person's conduct reprehensible," said Mr. Trench,

Ferguson's friend and next-door neighbor in a formal statement to a local newspaper. "Philip Ferguson is dead now. Why smear his memory with more mud and filth? His wife and family have already suffered enough."

Time was hanging by a hair's-breadth now. All it would take for the axe to fall was merely another phone call—and that same "anonymous tipster" was surely prepared to make it. As Dave walked to school on borrowed time that Monday morning, he could almost hear the soft insinuating voice. He could see the middle-aged, gray-haired figure of Dr. Corvo breathing into a phone. "Excuse me, Lieutenant, but could I make a suggestion? The husband of that woman who was killed. The schoolteacher, David Marks. *He* drives a cab now—drives one three or four nights a week. So possibly, just possibly, Lieutenant, he's the same man you're looking for, the same driver who was hanging around the Ferguson house in Connecticut."

The photographs, the descriptions by the neighbors would match perfectly. He could see Romano in some grubby office in Manhattan, assembling pictures and fingerprints from the cab company. He could see the older man's bloodshot eyes peering over the half-glasses, and in the background the black face of Officer Crandall, nodding solemnly . . .

As he walked into his classroom that morning, excited voices greeted him. He had thought these kids only looked at TV. He had thought they never read a newspaper. But here was Vince—

"Hey, was that your wife's pitcher in the paper . . ?"

"Yep." Dave picked up a piece of chalk.

"She got kilt on Fi't Avenoo?"

"That's right. Sit down, everybody."

"And you said dat—about dat guy—dat you'd *kill* him?" Harry asked, with his eyes lighting up.

Hands were waggling. Bodies were squirming, pushing and shoving against him. "Hey—d'ja ever look for him? Where'd you look for him? Mr. Marks. *Mr. Marks!*"

They had read and they had digested—perhaps already made the connection the police had not yet made. "D'ja ever see that dude, that Ferguson? D'ja know him? The one dat got kilt?"

Willie plucked at his sleeve, surprisingly bright and alert today. "D'ja ever go up there—*yourself*—to that guy's house?" He had become a celebrity, a glamorous figure, merely by being mentioned in the *Daily Witness* in connection with a murder. He was famous because he had a wife who had been battered into a pulp. "Will it be on television, Mr. Marks?" asked Dolores in a husky voice. She plucked at her bodice with dirty fingernails. Especially in the eyes of the big boys, the ones with mustaches, he could detect a new respect, even envy. The taint of crime, the association with violence had raised him a hundred percent in their eyes.

"No calls."

The alarm clock ticked on the refrigerator. The rain fell in Brooklyn. "She knows your number in Flatbush?" Momma asked for the tenth time. She was darning socks on the sofa.

"Yep."

"And your number at the cab company?" She bit off a thread.

"And at the school?"

"Yes." They were like people on a tightrope. They were people in a lifeboat in the middle of the sea. Momma's nails were bitten to the quick. They never left the phone unmanned for a single second. They never let anyone who called up talk for more than three minutes without ending the conversation. It was night and then it was morning again.

Mr. Kahn remained unconscious for day after day. He hovered between life and death. At night Dave drove feverishly past all the old places where he had seen Diana Roberts. In his spare time he phoned model agencies, restaurants, research foundations and supper clubs.

On Tuesday evening he stopped off at a synagogue and prayed for her to call him. He prayed she wasn't dead, or being held a prisoner.

On Wednesday after school he went again to the hospital to visit Mr. Kahn. The old man was still barely conscious, still curled in a vacuum world of hissing oxygen and glistening glucose tubes, but he opened his eyes when he heard Dave's voice and fixed them on Dave intensely.

With tiny liver-spotted hands he began to fumble with the

sheet, as though he were trying to throw it back, trying to get out of bed. Then he sank back against his pillows and pointed shakily to the wall.

"What is it, Mr. Kahn?"

Weakly the old man shook his head. He closed the pinched and sunken eyes.

But a moment later they opened again. With more agitation and strength, he squirmed and twisted in the high hospital bed and pointed toward the wall.

"What is it? What do you want?"

Against the wall stood a metal clothes locker. Dave opened its door as the old man continued to point. On two hooks inside hung the stained gray suit, the mended balbriggan underwear. In the jacket pocket of the suit was the black leather notebook.

"This is what you wanted?"

With a lump in his throat Dave heard Mr. Kahn's voice speaking to him for the first time in four days. It was weak, more like a squeak than a voice. "Yes."

"You want *me* to have it?"

For a moment Mr. Kahn's fragile hand rested on his wrist. It trembled. Mr. Kahn nodded. Then with a deep shuddering sigh he lay back against his pillows. He smiled faintly. He closed his eyes.

On the subway going home Dave began deciphering the spidery penmanship. He was so intent on reading, in fact, that he missed his station, and had to backtrack over drafty platforms and down stairs. Even to hold the notebook in his hand was like hearing the old man talk. It was like having him at his side, strong and well and skeptical again. It was like sharing his remarkable mind.

But if Dave was hoping for a miracle, he was sadly disappointed at first glance.

In spite of all the incredible research Mr. Kahn had done in New York and Connecticut, there was not one concrete conclusion to be found about the murderer of Philip Ferguson. There was nothing definitive about the identity and whereabouts of Diana Roberts. And nothing at all, not a word, on the subject of Dr. Wolfgang Corvo.

Yet Mr. Kahn had desperately wanted him to have the notebook. Why?

Again as the rain poured and night fell in the apartment, Dave sat in the dinette re-reading and pondering every word that Mr. Kahn had written.

There were dozens and dozens of facts, of course, on the subject of Philip Ferguson and his immediate circle. Mr. Kahn had researched the man as though he were researching the life of Napoleon. He had talked to servants, beauty parlor operators, Trench's secretary and Alexander Ferguson's buxom Portuguese cleaning woman. He had picked up all manner of oddments—such as the fact that Mrs. Ferguson liked the color and the scent of lavender and was a chain-smoker, and that once, on a bet, Robert Trench had held his breath under water in Ferguson's pond so long that he became unconscious and had to be taken to the hospital.

While Momma clattered the dishes and the boys whooped up and down the hall, Dave read of Philip Ferguson's gout which sometimes paralyzed him after too many martinis or too much love-making. He learned of Robert Trench's play that had failed on Broadway, Alexander Ferguson's pet python, "Lover Boy," and Sharon Ferguson's talent for piano-playing. She had performed "Tales from the Vienna Woods" in a teen-age beauty contest.

Dave kept turning pages, frowning, meditating.

The name of William Glaxton met his eye. William Glaxton was dying of cancer in a Norwalk hospital. Portia Ferguson had married again, her former agent Hyman Schneider, and had gone for treatment in her wheelchair to the Mayo Clinic in Rochester. When these pages were written, of course, on the last Saturday of his heart attack, Mr. Kahn had had no knowledge that the black MG had been found in the quarry. He did not know about the police's visit to Dave, or Dave's encounter with Diana at Coney Island.

"Corvo. Dr. Wolfgang Corvo, Ph.D." He had written down only the name. There was no other entry.

For some unknown reason, the last few items in the notebook had been concerned only with the backgrounds of those people Dave had seen or talked to on Red Mill Lane while he was waiting in his cab those three nights in Stamford.

On that bright breezy Saturday while Dave was flying a kite in Coney Island, Mr. Kahn had gone from Stamford to Westport, then all up and down Red Mill Lane, checking on Mrs. Harriet Shaw, the family of young Charles Miller, and the guests at the party at Trench's house that rainy night. He had spent considerable time trying to track down the middle-aged drunk who had asked Dave for a ride to Westport, and his girl friend Muffin, the one who had driven off in the red MG.

No one knew their names or had ever heard of them. No one knew who Muffin was, and no one remembered either one as having attended Trench's party. "Perhaps the scene was staged for a purpose," Mr. Kahn had written in a shaky hand, obviously on board the train coming back from Stamford just moments before his heart attack.

And then the words, "Connecticut is a sewer covered by green grass and pretty flowers," and still more shakily, "Imitation is not always . . . flattery."

The handwriting had trailed off. It had become more and more illegible, until at the very bottom of the page there was only one word which seemed to begin with a "C." The more Dave looked at it the more it resembled the name "Corvo." What did it mean? Why had Mr. Kahn written it in that particular context? Dave glued his eyes to the page. He turned the notebook in all directions.

The clock ticked. The rain fell. And Momma sat down with her sewing basket. In times of crisis, she always darned, but that night there wasn't a sock or a pair of small overalls left, and she kept turning and turning the tangled spools of thread, watching him with bright dark eyes.

The phone rang and they both dived for it. Dave picked it up, and when Momma saw his face, she closed her eyes. Tears started rolling down her cheeks.

"David? Is this David?" The beautiful voice was sharp, high-pitched. It sounded almost shrill. "I'm in the subway, David, and I'm ready to talk. I promise I will. I'm going with you to the police."

"Thank God," he said. "Where are you, Diana? I'll come anywhere you say." He could hear a subway train roaring in the distance, echoing. "Where?" he repeated.

"You—forgive me?" she cried thinly.

"Yes. *Where?*"

The train grew louder.

"Eddie's."

"Eddie's! Who's Eddie?"

"It's—a bar," she said. "On Fifty-first and Third." The train roared. "It's around the corner from a police station," she shouted. "Oh, David, don't be long."

He was already out the door.

Sixteen

Eddie's was halfway up the block when he came racing up Fifty-first Street from the Lexington Avenue subway. It had a blue flickering sign, a bow window with white café curtains, and inside it was long and narrow with a massive mahogany bar stretching along one wall, with wooden booths opposite. Stained-glass chandeliers cast strange green and yellow checkers of light on the people lined up along the bar or seated at the wooden tables along the walls.

There were two or three slender blondes with their backs toward him at the bar. None was Diana.

The booths had very high backs. They were all occupied except for one in the rear. He headed for it rapidly, then stopped, noticing the half-finished drink, the remains of a club sandwich and the pack of mentholated cigarettes on the bare table.

"It's taken." A pretty fair-haired waitress in minuscule pink shorts and a tank-top moved past him, balancing a tray heaped high with lobster shells on her shoulder.

"By a lady?" Dave asked.

"No, a gentleman."

The main dining room just beyond the drinking section was shadowy and empty. Light coming fitfully through a swinging door that led to a kitchen even farther beyond fell on red-checked tablecloths, empty chairs, and a sign marked MS. AND MR. Diana was nowhere visible.

Making his way back to the bar, Dave surveyed every face in

every booth. Then with a final glance around the noisy crowded room he went out and stood in the cold rain and the fresh air, looking up and down the sidewalk.

He was back in a couple of minutes.

"What'll it be?" the bartender asked.

Dave eased his body in through the press of other bodies.

"You see a blond girl?" he asked the bartender. "Long straight hair. Blue eyes. High cheekbones. Young."

The bartender looked like a fledgling Irish poet. He had high cheekbones and long reddish hair tied back in a ponytail, and he wore a huge striped apron of mattress ticking. On his nose were very small eyeglasses.

"Nope."

"I was supposed to meet her here," Dave said. "Her name's Diana Roberts."

"Who?"

"Diana Roberts."

The bartender looked at Dave thoughtfully. Pursing up his lips and sucking in his gaunt cheeks, he stared into space for a moment or two. "She might have worked here as a hostess or a waitress at one time," Dave said. "You wouldn't happen to know her?"

"Nope."

The bartender moved away. He waited on another customer. Dave took out a five-dollar bill. The bartender returned.

"What'll it be?" the bartender said.

"A beer."

Dave pushed the five dollars toward the bartender. As the bartender was pouring his beer he said, "You wouldn't happen to know her address, would you?"

"Nope."

"It's pretty important," Dave said, looking at him steadily. "*Any* information you could give me. She's been missing for a week, and she might be dead."

"Sorry."

The bartender wiped Dave's beer with a paper napkin. Then he looked at Dave sourly. "I've only worked here for a week, man, and tonight I'm quitting. It's strictly plastic here. I'm going back to Oklahoma."

The bartender moved away, and as Dave followed him with

his eyes, he noticed a man walking toward him down the aisle of booths, a man familiar, a man he had just been reading about in Mr. Kahn's black notebook.

He was Robert Trench.

When last seen he had been jogging down a country lane in the sunset nearly three weeks ago, with a tennis racket in his hand. Tonight he wore a tweed jacket and a gray turtleneck sweater over the collar of which his fair hair straggled. His double chin sagged. He looked tired, abstracted, out of sorts. A cigarette dangled from his mouth.

Pausing not far from Dave, he struck a match and lit the cigarette, his gaze traveling vaguely about the bar. It fixed on a passing waitress, a very thin waitress with red curls. Tapping her on the shoulder, as she started to go by him, he pointed to the empty booth at the rear and handed her some bills. She grinned, pocketed the money and curtsied mockingly. Grimacing, Trench ambled on.

Dave had stopped sipping his beer by then, and withdrawn toward the very front of the bar. He stood next to the big bow window with its white café curtains.

Trench came on steadily.

Dave kept waiting for him to open the restaurant's front door and step out into the rainy street.

But Trench had turned off at a phone booth just inside the front door.

As Dave watched from his post at the bow window, Trench closed the glass door of the booth, put a dime in and dialed.

As people came and went, occasionally blocking Dave's view completely, Trench began to talk earnestly on the phone, his handsome fleshy profile turned toward Dave and one hand gesturing. Once Trench frowned and stuck his lower lip out. And once his shoulders shook with silent laughter. But no matter what he did, his pale jaded face exuded a repellent quality. Trench looked cold, cynical—predatory. He looked old, too, far older than he had looked in Connecticut. His hair in the dim light seemed not blond, but gray.

"Middle-aged. Gray-haired," she had said. *"He took me to nice places . . . elegant restaurants. He seemed a highly intelligent, distinguished man."*

Trench hung up. Then he was walking out of the restaurant,

closing the front door behind him against the blowing rain and pausing in front of the bow window to light still another cigarette.

From over the white café curtains Dave watched him. Trench was looking at his watch, then glancing from right to left. Suddenly he disappeared from the bow window altogether. He was walking rapidly down the block.

Dave relaxed for a few seconds.

Again he scanned the place for Diana Roberts. It was now nearly ten o'clock. At least three-quarters of an hour had passed since his arrival and an hour and a half since she had called him up in Brooklyn. Once more he was seized by a feeling of panic, a feeling that once again she had lost her nerve or been bypassed by her nemesis, Corvo. As his eyes returned to the front door and the bow window, suddenly he saw Trench again, outside, barely a few feet away. Trench was standing on the sidewalk with his back to Dave not far from the bow window, and as Dave watched, Trench moved toward the curb with one hand lifted, as though he were hailing a cab.

But no cab was pulling over. Instead, it was a police car. As Dave watched, transfixed, for just one more split second, two cops got out and moved across the sidewalk toward Eddie's.

They swung open the front door.

By then Dave was running, moving swiftly past the booths, the blond and red-haired waitresses, plunging into the shadowy dining room and through the swinging doors into the kitchen.

"Hey, whassa matter wid you?" A giant man with a potbelly tried to grab him. Pots clanged and dishes crashed as Dave zigzagged across the steamy room, hearing shouts now from the body of the restaurant and a police whistle, the clatter of feet. More arms reached out to stop him, hands grabbed for his pants and windbreaker, but he dodged past stoves and overflowing garbage cans and jerked a screen door open. It confronted a dark yard glittering with broken glass and barricaded by a high board fence.

The whistle blew again as scuttling across the yard he hurled himself at the board fence, scrambled up and found it topped with barbed wire. As the shadows began running out of the lighted kitchen behind him, he threw himself over the fence and landed in a puddle. Lights played over dark walls and voices echoed as he ran, darting into a steep-walled narrow alley filled with trash and stinking filth, a ratlike passageway that went on and on between the skyscrapers and the tall elegant buildings that lined this fashionable street.

Finally he came out. He was at least a block away from Eddie's. Standing there panting, with his heart pounding, he could hear very faintly the sound of a police siren.

Dripping with sweat, he removed his windbreaker and wiped his bleeding hands with it. Then he dropped it into a trash can and started walking rapidly west. In a drugstore he bought a cheap razor and in the men's room of a seedy hotel near Columbus Circle he shaved off his mustache. It had been his vanity. Fran had loved it. It had belonged to another era when he had been a nice guy, a decent guy who had trusted people and tried to help them. But that era was long past.

In the men's room mirror his face looked naked, ugly, ruthless.

He dropped the razor in a wastebasket and walked out into the night.

In the fleet garage roaring with sound and heavy with gasoline fumes he moved like a thief, a shadow, along the greasy, oil-stained walls. In a far corner he found an old cab that was empty, but the ignition keys were in it and the radio worked. The gas tank was a quarter full.

He revved the engine, released the brake and headed full throttle for the open door. At top speed he passed the streetlamp and the dark warehouses, and headed for the Hudson River.

Seventeen

At a breakneck pace he drove to Connecticut, turning off at the exit for Red Mill Lane.

The white gateposts loomed out of the darkness. He drove past them, moving on up the hill to Trench's quaint red stable house with its silo in the rear. He slowed down. Trench's house was dark and the Thunderbird wasn't visible. Driving on up to the church, Dave parked his stolen cab in the graveyard under a tree. Then he walked downhill to the lane where at sunset on a warm spring evening three weeks before, he had seen Robert Trench jogging toward the barn-red house whose pretty white curtains had once reminded him of Fran.

Far below, the Ferguson property was dark, shrouded in rain and mist. He could not even see the roofs or the chimneys. He walked up Trench's narrow dirt lane.

The lane ended in a small flagstone patio bordered by a low stone wall. The wall overlooked a steep drop, a rocky cliff. Beneath it, far, far down, he could glimpse the black mist-hung water of the Ferguson pond.

Trench's property overhung the Ferguson property like the bowsprit of a ship. From here, from this projecting terrace halfway up the hill, a man, during the daylight hours, might be able to spy on almost anything happening below. On a clear still night he could probably hear almost anything that was being said on that lawn or around that pond.

Dave moved cautiously across the rain-wet flagstones. He peered through the plate glass doors leading from it into Trench's house.

The doors were sliding ones with snap locks. They did not budge. The room beyond was in darkness. He padded around the house a couple of times and finally found a window that shuddered upward when he pushed. It rose higher and higher and he crawled in silently—so sure of what he had come for and so outraged at the man himself that he did not hesitate to trespass for the second time at Red Mill Lane.

He had only to prove what seemed already obvious.

Robert Trench and "Dr. Wolfgang Corvo" were one and the same man.

Trench answered Diana's description. He had fair hair turning gray. He was middle-aged and fairly distinguished-looking. As an intellectual, a writer, he was perfectly capable of devising diabolical plots and complicated intrigues.

Trench had class, mobility, no ties, no wife or family to answer to. He lived alone. He was a bachelor. And Trench perhaps needed money—desperately. His play had failed. He had no reputation as an author. Although Trench professed to be Ferguson's friend, he undoubtedly despised Ferguson secretly. Ferguson was rich. Yet he had never done a day's work in his life. He owned boats, a tennis court, a bigger house, more property—and was a huge hit with the ladies. Very possibly Robert Trench was madly in love with Philip Ferguson's beautiful third wife.

All it had required to kindle the final spark in Trench's envious mind was for Trench to learn about the car accident. And how easy that must have been for a man who lived next door to Philip Ferguson.

On the dark night of October 16 or the chill dawn of October 17, Trench hád possibly glimpsed Ferguson sneaking home in his battered MG, then soon sneaking out again. Or Trench had run across Ferguson on the road, trudging home from the quarry on foot. Anything was possible, any encounter of any sort, but it was quite obvious to Dave that Trench must have known from the beginning that the MG was in the quarry and made it his business to find out why.

For a while perhaps, as Diana had intimated, Trench (or Corvo) might have been content merely to blackmail his old friend. But eventually tiring of that, he had decided on murder.

It was simpler. It posed more of a challenge. It would also ultimately free Sharon Ferguson and all her money—for Trench to pay court to once the mourning period was past.

So several months ago Trench had set off to New York and Eddie's—to hire a pretty young blond waitress, namely Diana Roberts, to assist him in his evil plot. Since then, under his fantastic pseudonym of Dr. Wolfgang Corvo, he had been scaring her and threatening her—and tonight, having gotten wind that she planned to meet Dave and go with him to the police, he had arrived at Eddie's first, frightened her away and waited for Dave himself. When Dave arrived, Trench had immediately phoned the cops and told them that their "chief suspect" was there.

The rain pattered on the bricks outside and drummed lightly on the roof. It was a small house, a simple house compared to the labyrinthine mansion down the hill. There were few rooms downstairs, all opening into one another. As Dave's eyes gradually became accustomed to the dark, he realized that these rooms consisted of a living room, a dining room, a breakfast nook and a small kitchen. He passed a bird chirping sleepily under a cover in a cage. He smelled the pungent odor of geraniums and the faint odor of fresh-baked bread. He had brought a flashlight along, but was not quite ready to risk turning it on. He kept listening, straining his ears for sounds. Up a winding, boxed-in flight of stairs he thought he heard a board creak. He thought he heard a footstep, the sound of a telephone being dialed. But then again there was total silence, except for the soft drip-drip of the rain.

Finally he snapped on the flashlight.

He was in a white-washed living room with a low ceiling, pine furniture and bright braided rugs scattered over the highly polished floor. Modern paintings, all of abstract design, decorated the walls. Pots of geraniums bloomed at the windows where crisp white curtains hung. And everywhere there were books—books jammed into book-shelves, piled up on chairs and tables, even stacked in cartons on the floor. His flashlight picked out a title: "*Charlemagne, Boy of the Middle Ages.* For Young Readers. By Robert Trench." And another: "*Alexander, Boy Emperor* by Robert Trench." And still another: "*Moose: A Tale of the North Woods.* For Young Readers. By Robert Trench in collaboration with Margaret Carson."

Dave frowned. The rain pattered. On a desk in a corner was a huge old-fashioned typewriter. Next to it pages of a thick manuscript were neatly piled. As he moved over to it with his flashlight, something rolled off the top of the manuscript pages. It fell to the floor and he picked it up.

It was a lipstick of pale lavender—the color of Sharon Ferguson's long dress.

He stood holding it, twirling it. Then he turned the flashlight beam on the pages of typed manuscript. On the top page was a neatly typed title: *"The U.S.S. Anaconda.* An Adventure of the Sea. For Young Readers. By Robert Trench."

On the second page, also beautifully typed, was a short paragraph.

> Based on a true-life story of the author's, this book is dedicated to the late Philip E. Ferguson who saved my life in World War II on a destroyer similar to the *U.S.S. Anaconda.*

Slowly Dave laid the page back on the manuscript. He turned the flashlight off for a moment. Yet he had to keep remembering Trench's flushed predatory face at Eddie's while he was making that call in the phone booth. And the gesture of command Trench had made as he crossed the rainy sidewalk, and the next minute the police car had come squealing over to the curb.

Dave stood frowning in the dark, fingering his naked upper lip, the bare spot where his mustache had been.

Trench had given the party that rainy night, the party which had produced the mysterious drunk and the girl named Muffin —plus all those other eager eyewitnesses.

Trench had been an eyewitness himself. He had been right there on the scene in his black Thunderbird that very first night Dave had driven Diana up to Red Mill Lane.

Dave clicked the flashlight on again.

He opened a desk drawer.

In the drawer were six sharpened yellow pencils, a box of paper clips, a postcard addressed to Miss Margaret Carson from Niagara Falls and signed "Love, Joe," and an address book of tooled Florentine leather.

Dave thumbed through the address book.

Under the R's there was a Lew Rosenfeld, a Larry Ruocco, a Leonard Rowans and a Jerry Ruppert, but no Diana Roberts. Among the C's, there was a Harry Clay, a Curley Carroway, a Barry Clews and a Bobo Cummings. But no Wolfgang Corvo. Most of the entries seemed to be men.

Dave stood frowning. Again he gazed around the pretty, cozy room. Then he clicked the flashlight off quickly. He listened.

Car wheels were coming up the lane. Headlights flashed across the walls. Dave moved toward a window. Outside, the Thunderbird was lurching to a halt. A car door slammed. Then he saw the figure of Trench in turtleneck sweater and tweed jacket advancing toward the glass doors of the patio. Trench was walking unsteadily. And he was not alone.

"Damn decent, Bunny," Dave heard him say in a thick slurred baritone as he fumbled for his keys. "Damn lonely here."

His companion Dave could not quite see. Trench was sliding a glass door open, blocking Dave's full view of the patio.

"Boring." Trench was mumbling.

He stepped in.

"Maggie! Mag!" he called.

His voice reverberated through the cold, still air. The rain had stopped. Dave could see the stars above the low stone wall, the rocky precipice.

"Mag—you still around?"

Trench was turning to address his invisible companion. "Damned conscientious—works all night. *Too* conscientious." He laughed foolishly. "Come on in."

He snapped on a light, and stood flushed and weaving on the threshold. His fair graying hair was tousled, dank, his eyes vague, his features slack. "Used to like that joint—that Eddie's." He stumbled into the room, steadying himself on an old pine hutch. "But tonight, I'm telling you, buddy—it was like a tomb."

"Yeah. Right." A slight young man came gliding in.

"You bet it was. I wen' down there to celebrate Phil's birthday. Old Phil. Always celebrated with him. Every year. Old Phil."

"Sure," the young man said. He wore a pea jacket and had dark curly hair. "You told me on the phone already. Remember?"

"Oh. Sorry," Trench replied.

"It's okay, Bob." The young man smiled.

"Don't want to repeat myself."

"You're not repeating yourself."

"I'm not?" Trench smiled. The young man smiled back at him. And for a minute or two, like two Cheshire cats in the dim glow of a green student lamp, they stood smiling at one another.

Dave began edging toward the patio.

"I can still miss him, though," Trench said to the young man. "Do you know he saved my life one time—the old bastard? *Saved* me!" He struck his fist against the palm of his hand and staggered backward against the wall. "Pulled me right out of the sea!"

"Did he now?" the young man said.

"Ship was on fire. Old Phil jumped in the water. Believe it or not"—Trench's voice was maudlin, but sincere—"you don't forget a guy like that."

"No, you don't, Bob."

Gracefully, lissomely the young man glided over to Trench. He draped an arm over the older man's shoulder.

"But I'm here now," he said softly.

Dave slid out the glass door into the patio. Then he ran down the lane and up the starlit hill.

116

Eighteen

In the early light of dawn Dave propped the paper against the
steering wheel and stared at the headlines and his photograph
on the front page.

The first rays of the sun were slanting against the canyon
walls, glittering on tenement windows, tinting the cobblestones.
With perspiring hands he steadied the paper and read:

> David Marks, a twenty-eight-year-old Brooklyn schoolteacher
> who took up taxi-driving after his wife's death, is being sought in
> connection with the murder of wealthy Connecticut textiles scion
> Philip E. Ferguson, according to homicide detectives.
>
> Police have identified Marks as the New York cabdriver who
> was observed by neighbors at the entrance to the Ferguson estate
> on at least three occasions, the last being the night of the Ferguson
> murder. Marks' wife was killed last October in a hit-and-run
> accident in Manhattan, and Marks, who was himself injured in the
> same accident, identified the hit-and-run car as a black MG driven
> by a gray-haired man wearing a patch over his left eye. Crazed
> with grief, Marks vowed at the time, police said, "to find the driver
> and kill him if it takes the rest of my life."
>
> Philip Ferguson, aged fifty-four, and gray-haired, was blind in
> the left eye and often wore an eye patch. He owned a black MG
> which was recently found in derelict condition in a weed-grown

117

quarry half a mile from his home. According to an anonymous caller, it had been in a hit-and-run accident on October 16 of last year and had killed a woman. Marks, when shown a picture of Ferguson, identified him as the man who had killed Mrs. Marks. Footprints and fingerprints found in the Ferguson home after the fatal shooting have been identified as those of David Marks who, police believe, broke into the Ferguson library and shot the fifty-four-year-old sportsman after luring him home from Florida with a long-distance call sent by ship-to-shore the night before.

David Marks, the father of two small children, who still retained his job in a Brooklyn junior high school in addition to driving a cab at night, was not at home when police arrived at his Flatbush apartment last night. Later he was reported as being in an East Fifty-first Street bar in Manhattan, but fled the scene when police arrived there. He is reputedly driving a cab from his cab company which he took from the garage at 11:30 P.M. last night . . .

Dave crumpled the newspaper and tossed it on the floor. "Bastards. Stupid bastards!" Blindly he stared out through his dirty windshield. Halfway down the block two kids were throwing a ball against a wall, wiry silhouettes against the light.

Breathing hard, he picked up the newspaper again and smoothed it out over his knee. He studied his photograph. It was a lousy one—his hack license photo, taken two months after Fran's death. His face looked dull, brooding and ominous.

Across his chest his license number was stamped—like a photo in a rogues' gallery.

"Bastards. *Diabolical* bastards!"

Then he saw her. She was coming toward him in the early morning light.

Misshapen in the bulky tweedy coat, her head molded by a scarf tied beneath her chin, she was hurrying along, shopping bag in hand, then stopping to peer carefully at his cab, eyes narrowed behind their spectacles.

"Momma—" Through the open window he called her name, and then leaned across the seat to open the door. As she climbed in heavily, she stared at him. "What's happened to your face?" she frowned.

"My mustache? I shaved it off."

"Oh, David, David . . ."

He started the cab, moving slowly down the empty streets of Flatbush. "Are the cops still there?" he asked.

"No, they've gone. But this is wrong, Dave, it's crazy."

"There's no other way, Momma."

She started to protest. "Shh," he said gently, glancing at her bulky body, her weary face. "Shh, Momma. Did you bring the money?"

"Twenty-three dollars." She unsnapped the worn pocketbook. "All I had in the house—plus what Fox could spare me."

"It's fine. What else did you bring me?"

The shopping bag lay on the floor at her feet. "Your sweater, like you told me. And some sandwiches, a coupla hard-boiled eggs, a thermos of coffee, a chocolate bar."

"Thanks, Momma," he said huskily. "Thanks."

"And the notebook. I thought you might need it."

"Wonderful."

Slowly he continued to circle the familiar streets. The sun was filling them with light, dazzling on the storefronts with their iron gates in front.

"That girl will be the death of you," she said.

"No, she won't, Momma. Don't say that."

"Hah! What a no-good. She called up the police. She led you into a trap."

"Not necessarily, Momma."

"Not *necessarily!*"

She laughed bitterly. "Oh, poor Dave. You really are crazy about her. If she told you the moon was green cheese, you'd believe her. If she asked you to meet her at the electric chair, you'd go, just as fast as your legs would carry you."

"Momma, lay off."

"Dave, give up on her."

"Momma, listen—"

"So, I'm listening."

"Maybe she just couldn't make it last night after she called me. Or she got there and saw Trench. Or she was late," he finished lamely.

"Phooey."

"I can't jump to conclusions. It's too complicated a case."

Dave drove past his school, bleak and silent in the morning

light. "I made one mistake last night. I can't go around accusing people—willy-nilly."

"Phooey," she said again.

She tossed her head in its black scarf. She twisted her fingers in their worn brown gloves. "It's the last time I'll ever see you," she mourned. "I just know it. Something terrible's going to happen to you."

Before he could interrupt, she addressed a Lerner's window they were passing. "And what will become of your boys then, your poor sons? When you're still running around looking for that no-good *shiksa*—in a cab you stole from the cab company. She's even made you into a thief."

"Momma, quit it," he said.

"I'll raise them for you, I'll do my best, an old woman. I'll tell them their father was a good man, a fine man, a schoolteacher. But he ruined his life by falling in love with a bleached blonde in a wig."

"What do you mean—a wig?"

"In a taxi," she intoned, "he caught his death of cold running around, not bothering to sleep." She broke off. "Dave, how can you ever find her? Where are you going to look? It's a big city with millions of people . . . and all she's told you about herself is just a bunch of lies."

"I can only try," he said. "She's my only chance now, Momma. I'm practically convicted by the newspapers. Everyone is sure I did it."

"Oh, my God, I don't believe that for a minute." She drew in her breath. "None of the neighbors think so. Fox doesn't think so. Look, Dave." She reached for his hand. "Kahn will get better. He can help us. We'll get lawyers, *good* lawyers. They can't railroad you like that."

"Momma, just relax," he said. "Just trust me." He patted her hand. "Momma, I love you."

"You love only that *shiksa*."

"Momma, cut it out. I love *you*. I love my boys. And I love—Fran."

She answered with a moan. Her breath caught in her throat. He had completed the circuit and was pulling up to the curb in front of the huge housing development where he had picked her up.

"Goodbye, Momma. Thanks, Momma."

"Dave, call me. Don't do anything crazy. Keep in touch," she said.

"I'll try."

She still lingered on the sidewalk. "I didn't mean to hurt your feelings. You're such a good boy with such a big heart. You've gotten hurt already so much."

"I'll be all right. Don't worry."

"I'll pray for you." Her lips began to quiver. "I'll pray for Fran to help you." She began to walk away. "Put on your sweater, for God's sake. You're shivering."

Then she was hurrying down the street toward the corner round which she had come. She rounded it. She did not look back.

Nineteen

Jim Flaherty, the chief dispatcher, was a man Dave liked. Gruff, hard-working, hard-boiled, he was the father of five kids, as well as two Korean war orphans he and his wife had adopted. He knew about the car accident and had always been friendly to Dave. Jim was on duty that morning. As soon as Momma disappeared, Dave clicked his two-way radio on.

Against a background of crisscross voices and scratchy electronics, he spoke into the small receiver.

"Jim . . . Jim, this is Dave Marks."

For a second or two there was no answer. When Flaherty replied, his voice was guarded.

"Yeah, Dave."

"You read the papers? You know about me?"

"Yeah, Dave," Jim rasped after a pause. "And you made off with the cab. The cops have been to see us. We know everything about you. So where are you now, kid?"

"I can't tell you, Jim."

Jim was silent. Then he said softly, "Better come in, son."

"I didn't do it," Dave said. "Jim, I'm innocent. I didn't murder Ferguson. I didn't even know him. You've got to believe me."

There was silence, then rasping static, and then the faint sound of another driver's voice. "Jim, I'm at La Guardia."

"Jim," Dave said, "are you still there?"

"Yeah, Dave."

"You've got to believe me," Dave said again.

"Okay, so I believe you, but that won't cut any ice with the cops. Come in and talk to them," Jim said.

"Nope, I'm not going to—right now."

"You realize that's a stolen cab you're driving—technically," Jim said.

"Yeah, I realize it—technically. I had to have it," Dave replied. Out of the corner of his eye he glimpsed a cop car coming toward him, and stepped on the gas. "I need help, Jim. Please, for God's sake, help me." He drove on, turning corner after corner, picking up speed, watching for the cop car to reappear in his rear-view mirror.

"The best thing you can do is come in right now," Jim was saying. "Hell, nobody blames you around here. If that son of a bitch had done that to my wife, I'd have done the same thing myself."

"Jim, I didn't kill him. I was framed," Dave said, as he sped along the Brooklyn Beltway past the warehouses of the Bush Terminal. "I was hired to go up to Stamford by this beautiful blond chick. She picked me up on the sidewalk. Three times I took her up there and I faked the trip sheets and I'm sorry. I was a damn fool idiot." He fell in between two trucks. "But she's the only alibi I've got, Jim, and I've got to find her. Otherwise I'm a dead pigeon. They set me up, Jim. You've got to believe me."

Static from the set grated in his ears, mingled with the rumble of morning traffic. And he could imagine Jim's face in the glass cubicle at the fleet garage, with the cigar stub hanging from his mouth and a frown creasing his freckled forehead.

Finally Jim said gruffly, "So what do you want me to do, kid?"

"Help me find her," Dave said. "Send out her description, broadcast it to the other guys, and if they spot somebody who looks like her, let me know quick. Okay? She's somewhere in this city, Jim, and I can't be everyplace at once. I can't watch all the hotels and terminals."

Silence. The set sounded dead for a minute. Dave fiddled with it. He shouted, "Jim!"

"Yeah," Jim said quietly.

"I can't go to the police about her. They won't believe me. I've got to find her—*physically* produce her—and make her talk, make her back me up."

"Yeah," Jim said. "I get the picture."

"She may call me—on a bare chance. At the garage. We used a signal. She'll say she's my sister, it's an emergency. Then she'll show up at the East Side Airlines Terminal."

"Yeah? That's some signal."

"It was nuts, Jim. I was stupid," Dave said. "Look—all I'm asking is for the other drivers to keep their eyes and ears open, and I'll do the rest. Hell, we're the best detectives in the city, Jim. We go everywhere, we see everything."

"That's true," Jim said. "You're right about that."

"I've got to find her." Dave again spoke urgently. "It's my only chance, my last chance. I'm not even sure of her name. I don't know where she lives—or one damned thing about her."

A minute passed.

"Jim?"

Then Jim came back on. "Okay, Dave, what's this chick look like?"

At eight that Monday morning it began. Behind the backs of the police, or under their very noses, the search started, the network formed, the noose was drawn. Operation Needle in Haystack, Jim called it—or by its code name ONH. Quietly, unobtrusively Flaherty passed the word about Dave Marks' dilemma to driver after driver, either over his intercom or at the garage itself. It filtered down to others. It even reached some of the gypsy drivers. And most of the men were sympathetic. For it was a cabdriver's story. It might have happened to any one of them.

Although thousands of them, of course, did not participate, and many of them undoubtedly sneered at Dave's naïveté and gullibility, not one of them betrayed the operation either—while it was going on. They felt too sorry for him. Dave had lost his wife in a terrible automobile accident and now was being accused of a murder he had not committed. Life had handed him an unusually raw deal—and they knew about raw deals. They had been handed plenty of raw deals, which was why many of them were driving taxis in the first place.

Dave hence became a secret cause—his search for Diana Roberts a kind of game, a challenge. And no one could have been better at the game than these sharp-eyed men, trained to scan every sidewalk for fares, every doorway, every entrance for possible passengers. Cruising everywhere, invading every street from the poorest to the most fashionable, shuttling from railroad station to airport, covering restaurants, hotels, office buildings and hospitals, they were the eyes and ears of the city twenty-four hours a day. They were a vast shifting web in which the most elusive butterfly might be caught.

"Blonde, between twenty-five and thirty," Dave had described her to Jim and Jim passed the description along. "Has long blond hair, blue eyes, high cheekbones and a super-refined voice. Wears boots and a long black coat. May carry a white umbrella or wear a black scarf or black turban. Smokes mentholated cigarettes. Frequents the West Fifties, the streets near Central Park. May possibly be in the company of a middle-aged man with graying hair."

Nothing happened all that day. Dave roamed the streets. He cruised past her old haunts. He watched for cop cars and ate Momma's sandwiches. Drinking coffee from Momma's thermos, he reread Mr. Kahn's notebook, still puzzling over that final entry, that name that looked like Corvo. The sun beat down on the hot sidewalks, and the old man was still incommunicado, still unable to talk, the hospital said. And on the radio, every hour on the hour, the newscasters kept talking about the "grief-crazed cabdriver" and the "bizarre" murder he had perpetrated on the man who had murdered his wife.

And then at six P.M. that evening a guarded voice came through the intercom. "Hey, Jim . . . Malakoff. ONH, Jim. I think I got a lead. This broad . . . a perfect match . . . she just went in to the Club Six."

"Dave?"

"I heard it, Jim."

Dave swung the steering wheel. He struggled crosstown through the evening traffic to the Club Six, a chichi restaurant with French décor and a pink striped canopy. Leaving the cab double-parked in front of the canopy he ran into the restaurant, wearing the old khaki sweater Momma had brought him that morning. A maître d' hurried over, all starched shirt front and consternation. Dave brushed past the maître d'. He strode past

125

grapes piled in silver baskets, wine bottles, pastry carts and frowning waiters into a glittering room of silver mirrors, pink tablecloths and crystal chandeliers. With her back to him a girl was seated talking to a gray-haired man with a gray goatee. She had long platinum hair undulating over a black silk coat. But she wasn't Diana. Her baby-blue eyes were wide and blank.

"Sorry, miss."

"Now listen, my good man . . ."

As he ran out of the restaurant, he saw two cops walking up the block toward his double-parked cab. Leaping in, he jammed down on the gas pedal, careened off and didn't stop till he was safely in Spanish Harlem.

"How'd it go, Dave?" Jim rasped.

"Wrong girl."

"Okay, kid, we'll keep trying."

"O–N–H . . . O–N–H."

By midnight he had checked out at least six other Dianas. He had also seen her himself—or fancied he had seen her—at least three times in the mid-Manhattan area.

Although boots and ankle-length coats were not stylish any more, corn-silk hair worn very long and straight was still extraordinarily prevalent. Her type was legion in New York.

At nine o'clock that evening he saw her dressed in blue jeans tripping down the steps of St. Patrick's floodlit cathedral on the arm of a bearded youth in blue jeans. At ten, clad in flapping gray bell-bottoms she was rounding a corner near the United Nations, behind a straining poodle on a leash. And at eleven, for a few seconds he was positive he saw her emerging from a Second Avenue delicatessen, dressed in a red fox jacket with two bags of groceries in her arms.

The leads he got that night from Jim and his fellow drivers included a girl from the chorus line at Radio City, a prostitute— and a transvestite.

Yet to him she had been special—a unique girl with a unique slant to her face. He knew he would recognize her anywhere, no matter how often her hair, her eyelashes, her clothes might be varied from the ones he had known. She had had a look of refinement—and great sadness. She had had a voice like a delicate clock chiming. Her face had not really been beautiful at

126

all times, but there had been something very wistful and appealing about it. Yet how could he tell that to Jim or the other drivers? How could he explain her mysterious attraction—the hold she had had from the beginning over his heart?

He slept that night in his cab, sprawled on the back seat, face pressed against the worn upholstery. He kept all four doors locked. When he woke at seven the next morning, rain was drumming on the cab roof, darkening the dismal buildings of Hudson Street and the long line of trucks waiting to enter the Holland Tunnel. The night dispatcher had no news for him. And on the radio he heard that Alexander Ferguson, brother of the slain man, was offering a ten-thousand-dollar reward for information leading to the whereabouts of David Marks.

He snapped the radio off.

He ate the half-melted chocolate bar, all that remained of the food Momma had given him, drank the dregs of her stale coffee, and stiff-legged and stiff-shouldered, dragged his way into a gas station. In the men's room mirror over the filthy sink he looked like a drunk, a guy from Skid Row, with black stubble sprouting all over his face, his hair greasy and disheveled, his eyes blurred.

Next to the broken coke machine there was a wall telephone. He put a dime in.

"Momma?"

"Dave, where *are* you?"

"Any calls, Momma?"

"No calls. Dave, come home. Don't keep on. Dave, she's never gonna call you. It's a waste."

In the background he could hear Jeremy singing, "Mary had a little lamb."

"Dave, it's crazy. Dave, please answer me."

"Its feece wuh white as snow," sang Jeremy.

"Dave."

He couldn't answer. There was a lump in his throat.

"Dave, come home. Give up. Go to the police."

"The—kids okay?" he finally asked.

"They're fine. She cheated you. She lied to you."

"And Mr. Kahn?"

"Better. We'll help you, Dave. We love you."

127

Slowly he hung up.

With tears welling in his eyes and Jeremy's voice still ringing in his ears, he left the filling station and returned to his cab. And yet he couldn't give up now. He couldn't, in all conscience. The search for Diana had become an obsession, he knew, but it was more than merely the need to get himself off the hook, and even more than merely a neurotic attachment, some weird desire to protect her. His crusade went much deeper. He had an almost superstitious feeling that if he gave up this search, if he stopped looking for her, he would be giving in completely to evil. His life would be forever blighted and accursed.

The rain danced on the cobblestones. It dashed against his streaming windshield—and he knew he had to break free of the chains which had been shackling him for over half a year. They had been put upon him that dark and terrible night in October, but he had to tear them loose, be free of all this morbidity and misery. He had to start a brand-new life. Maybe leave Brooklyn. Leave schoolteaching. Move out west. Seek new horizons for himself, and brighter, better vistas for his two little boys.

He thought of Joel's red kite dancing ever higher in the sky. And Jeremy smiling at the sea, and sifting sand in his small fists.

"Its feece wuh white as snow."

He sat behind the steamy windshield with tears still filling his eyes, until the streets, the buildings became a blur, veiled by water, a city under the sea.

Then he clicked the intercom on and splashed off into the rain.

It rained all day. No messages came through. Traffic crawled through the streets, bodies were veiled by raincoats and hidden under umbrellas. Dave spent the day making a huge final pitch to find Dr. Wolfgang Corvo. To find Corvo was to find Diana. He ended up in Mr. Kahn's old bailiwick, the New York Public Library. At two o'clock he entered the main reading room.

Service was slow. He had to wait a long time for every book he ordered. In *Who's Who* no Wolfgang Corvo was listed. He was not in *Who's Who in Science* or *Famous Living Scientists*, nor was his name in any of the five or six other volumes dealing with notable research projects by American scientists.

"Have you a list of Ph.D.'s?" Leaning in his damp khaki

sweater over the desk in the main catalog room, he asked the young clerk who'd been helping him. She consulted an index, left, and ten minutes later, returned to say that the list was missing from the stacks.

"Well, thank you very much, miss." It was five o'clock. He left the huge echoing marble building. The skies were still dark, the rain falling in fitful squalls. A wild wind had sprung up and he was drenched from head to foot as he made his way back against the wind to the West Side junkyard where he had parked the cab.

He was dying of hunger. He had eaten nothing since Momma's chocolate bar. Stopping off at a tiny luncheonette near Tenth Avenue, he wolfed down a hot meat-loaf sandwich. As he waited for a second cup of coffee, his eye fell on a brand-new phone book hanging from a chain next to the counter, and on a whim he started leafing through it. There were at least ten Corvos listed in this Manhattan directory alone. None was named Wolfgang.

From the waitress he got a dollar's worth of dimes and went to work.

The first two numbers did not answer. The third call was answered by a thick male voice.

"I'm looking for a Dr. Wolfgang Corvo," Dave said. "A distinguished scientist. I wonder if you can tell me whether he's a member of your family . . . a relative."

"Dunno," was the reply. "Don't know nuttin'." The receiver was jammed down.

On the fifth dime Dave got a shrill woman who said she had no use for any of the Corvos, they were all a bunch of kooks and harpies. A child answered the seventh call. On the eighth he finally found a woman who sounded reasonably friendly and intelligent.

"Yes, this is Mrs. Corvo," she said pleasantly. "Wolfgang? Did you say *Wolfgang*?" She laughed. "Are you serious?"

"Yes," Dave said. "He's not listed in the phone book and I'm anxious to get in touch with him. He's a scientist, a Ph.D."

The woman was laughing again. "Are you sure someone's not pulling your leg, sir? *Wolfgang Corvo, Doctor Wolfgang Corvo!*" Again she giggled. "He was a character on a kiddies' program about two or three years ago—on TV in Chicago. We're from

129

Chicago, and my kids were crazy about him. A kind of poor man's Captain Kangaroo."

"Oh," said Dave.

He sagged against the wall.

"It didn't go over with the general public. It was mainly local—just around the Great Lakes. But Wolfgang was adorable. He was supposed to be some funny little freaked-out scientist with pop eyes and a crazy accent and a huge bow tie. He ran a research lab in outer space and did all sorts of crazy experiments." She laughed. "Wolfgang Corvo. I adored him. Is the show going to be revived?"

"No, ma'am."

He sat stirring his lukewarm cup of coffee, not drinking it for a long, long time after he hung up. Then on leaden feet he plodded onward to his cab.

The sky was clearing, the rain had stopped, and in the west the sun was sinking in great windy swirls of red and orange. He climbed into the cab and sat with chin sunken on his chest, his shoulders slumped forward, and for a long time did not turn the intercom on. The taxi smelled of mildew and sweat. It smelled of stale clothes and staler hopes. It was littered with paper cups, old newspapers, chocolate bar wrappers, Momma's crumpled shopping bag and Mr. Kahn's soiled, limp notebook. But Dave didn't open a window. He didn't move. He simply sat there feeling a sense of utter desolation, a self-hatred, a disgust—for having been deceived so easily, so flagrantly and for so long.

"Bitch. Filthy . . . lying *bitch!*"

He said it for the first time.

The words still choked in his throat.

She had not been anybody's accomplice.

She had not been paid. She had not been hired. She had not been scared—for there had never been any Dr. Corvo to scare her. She had done the whole thing alone. And he knew it now, he could feel it, as though a trap door had just been sprung beneath his feet.

"Dave?"

"Yes, Jim."

It was seven o'clock and nearly dark before he finally turned

130

the intercom on. He was still sitting next to the junkyard, watching the traffic whiz over the West Side Highway.

"Dave, for God's sake," Jim barked amidst static. "Where you been, kid? I've been calling you for hours."

"I'm coming in, Jim."

"Whaddaya mean?"

"I'm coming in. I'm giving up. It's hopeless. I'll never find her."

There was a short silence. "But we found her," Jim said. "She isn't far from here."

"Where?"

"She's standing on a streetcorner—half a block from the garage. The hair, the boots, the coat. She's standing under a street lamp."

"Come on."

"It's true, kid."

"By herself?" Dave asked.

"Yes," Jim said.

"Since when?"

Dave was shaking. Cold chills were moving up and down his body.

"About ten minutes," Jim said. "One of the drivers just brought her over—from the Barbizon-Plaza Hotel."

"Oh, my God."

Dave put his head down for a moment on the steering wheel. It felt cold, ice-cold, drenched with sweat—his sweat.

"So what do you want us to do, kid?" Jim said softly.

"Has she called me? Used the signal?"

"No," Jim replied.

The static crackled—inhumanly. The West Side Highway traffic flashed by. "It's got to be her, Dave." Jim's voice emerged from the static again. "Why don't you just take a look at least? Then you can give up. The boys will be disappointed."

"O–kay."

"What have you got to lose?"

"Okay."

As he turned the ignition key, he saw the moon just beginning to rise over his left shoulder. It was almost full. It seemed to watch him as he headed toward the fleet garage, the dark warehouses, the street lamp.

Twenty

There was no one in the circle of light cast by the street lamp. Not a shadow moved on the long dark lonely street.

Everything seemed strangely silent. The old gloomy warehouses stretched toward the Hudson in the dim light of the rising moon. Toward the east the lighted cliffs of the New York skyline glittered. Then his scalp prickled. From the direction of the river a police car was approaching. He could see its red light flashing like fire two blocks away. It moved toward him swiftly, with its siren just beginning to sound.

At the same time another police car glided toward him from the direction of the fleet garage. With siren beeping, rising, in nerve-racking cacophony to the other siren, it came closer—and in panic he ground down on the accelerator. He spun the wheel.

The engine faltered, then roared as the old cab lurched forward. With both sirens wailing louder and louder and red lights flashing brightly behind him, he fled the scene—like any common criminal, a fugitive.

Round corners, up curbs, along sidewalks he raced, with tires squealing and the twin sirens in full pursuit behind him now. The moon reeled, the tenements swayed, and the city lights were blurs before his eyes. A line of garbage cans clattered and went rolling every which way in the path of his pursuers. A cat fled and pedestrians scattered as blowing his horn and gripping the steering wheel he went hurtling down dark narrow streets and finally reached an avenue full of traffic, in which he lost himself.

Among all the other yellow cabs cruising in a steady stream he was safe, anonymous for the time being—and the sirens faded to nothing. But he was far uptown before he dared to come to rest—and then he turned into a huge asphalt parking lot filled with empty Greyhound buses. Here, amidst these behemoths of the road, lined up like elephants in the light of the moon, he stopped, turned off the engine and lay sidelong on the front seat.

Sweat bathed his body. His heart was pounding. His shirt clung to him like a wet layer of skin. Even his sweater was moist with perspiration.

"Dave . . . Dave." The idiot intercom was still crackling. In the silence Jim's voice could again be heard.

"Dave? You okay? Dave, I'm sorry. She left the lamppost five minutes before you got there—and the next thing the cops took over," Jim said.

Dave did not answer.

"Dave?" Jim rasped hoarsely.

Dave picked up a newspaper and started wiping his neck with it. He rolled a window down. In the moonlight the gray buses loomed above him and a cool breeze blew in.

"Dave—she's in a cab on her way downtown," Jim said. "We've still got her covered. We'll let you know where she ends up."

Dave gulped fresh air.

"Okay, Dave?"

"Okay, Jim."

"Roger," Jim said. And Dave could tell by the sound of his voice how relieved Jim was. "It's *got* to be her, Dave, for sure."

"Yeah, if the cops showed up, it's her," Dave said.

"Okay, so we've got two guys tailing her." Jim broke off. "Wait a second." Jargon and jumbled sound ensued. "Dave"—Jim's voice came back on—"she just got off at the Barbizon-Plaza."

"Which entrance?"

"Fifty-eighth Street."

Dave sighed. "If she's in that hotel she'll just walk out again—through the Fifty-ninth Street entrance. She doesn't live there, she just uses it as an escape hatch," he said.

. "*Wait* a minute," Jim said.

Dave waited.

Jim's voice was jubilant. "She's just come out. One of our guys just saw her—on the Fifty-ninth Street side. And she's walking up the block toward Columbus Circle."

"Alone?"

"Yeah, but picking up speed. Better hot-foot it over here," Jim said. Dave was already pulling out of the bus parking lot. "Hey. She's stopping off at a phone booth."

"Okay, I'm on my way."

He started downtown, still half unable to believe it. The system was working perfectly. It seemed a miracle. Here he was, speeding in his cab, miles from target, and yet not a move Diana was making, not a step that she was taking was unknown to him, thanks to ONH and Jim Flaherty—and those hawk-eyes watching from their cab windows over on Fifty-ninth Street near Central Park.

He could practically see her—see the coat swinging and the long hair floating as she hurried along and turned in at that glass phone booth, undoubtedly all unaware that she was the focus of a search by thousands of men who had been scanning the streets for her for two days and a night.

"Hey, Dave!" Half laughing Jim was paging him again. "Guess who just phoned you. *She* did. On the signal. She said she was your sister, she was sick, it was an emergency."

"Thanks."

Dave was now on Ninety-sixth Street, flying along Riverside Drive.

"Meanwhile I just got word from Malakoff. He's in the East Side Terminal vicinity. And he says a cop car just stopped in front of the terminal building. They've pulled up a little ahead of the entrance."

"Thanks, Jim."

"She's some operator."

Dave passed Seventy-second Street. He sped through a red light. "Where's she now?"

"Walking up Fifty-ninth Street. Still on her way to the Circle."

Dave plunged into Central Park, taking the short cut to the Fifty-ninth Street exit through winding roads and greenery. Jim was giving him minute-to-minute bulletins now. Diana had turned left. She was hurrying downtown along Sixth Avenue. She had reached Fifty-eighth Street and Dave was almost out of the park and scanning the streets ahead with frantic eyes when

Jim suddenly broke off. Dave heard him say "Hell!" Then there was silence.

"What's the matter?"

"She just went down the damn subway stairs—at Fifty-seventh and Sixth."

After a while Jim said wearily. "Look, maybe there's a chance we can head her off."

"Head her off? How?"

"That's a terminal station. All the uptown trains stop there. Then they go back downtown," Jim said. "So—she's got to be on a downtown train."

"So you mean I could keep up with her," Dave said, "and watch all the stops to see if she comes out?"

"Nope," Jim barked. "The team." Then he went off the intercom for a few minutes. "Okay." He came back on. "I got guys from here to Manhattan Bridge posted along the subway, every stop, local and express. It's a cinch. She can't possibly get away."

"So where do I come in?"

"Start moving downtown along the subway route. Keep on moving, and we'll be in touch with you."

"Thanks, Jim. Sure. That's great."

But Dave felt no hope at all, as he started toward Times Square.

The New York subway system was a vast network of interlocking lines which spread in a tangled underground of tracks and stations all over the five boroughs, and it was possible to travel for miles in all directions, change subway systems and even enter stores, hotels, office buildings and railroad stations without ever coming up for air, without ever being seen by eyes above the surface.

In the subway Diana was lost to him—as quickly as though she'd plummeted into hell. He could never hope to pursue her, never hope to find her—and once again a wave of hopelessness seized him, a feeling that something evil, something inhuman had him in its grip. He could never get free of the nightmare. He must live forever with misery. She was unreal, a phantom, a ghostly dybbuk whom he must eternally seek and never find.

"La belle dame sans merci hath thee in thrall."

He kept driving, driving—past the lighted theaters, past Macy's, above that dark world below . . .

"Dave! She's surfaced! She's out."

Jim's voice rang through the cab, and instantly Dave's despair left him. He came immediately to life.

"Where?"

"Never mind where!" Jim was hoarse with excitement. "She's at the Ace Parking Lot. Eighth near Sixth. The Village."

"Thanks. Thanks for everything."

"If you need help, call us."

Dave squealed around a corner.

He plunged into the maze of narrow, twisting crowded streets that constituted Greenwich Village. Progress was slow. On this moonlit night in April every block he entered was jammed with long-haired, blue-jeaned young people drifting from honky-tonk to honky-tonk as though they were attending a party.

Lights glowed from bizarre storefronts. Rock music assailed his ears. But the Ace Parking Lot appeared to be deserted, a dark narrow slot of a parking lot between an adult movie house and a sidewalk café. He drove up to it, slowing down for more hordes of pedestrians. He could see no cars, no attendant, no Diana.

But even as he lingered for a moment near the curb, he spied headlights, and a car lurched out of the lot from the shadows at the rear. It paused briefly before pulling out into traffic.

It was a red MG.

In the front seat sat Diana, her face pale and grim in a black scarf.

Then the car shot forward. It turned left.

Low-slung, black-hooded, like some small but deadly bug, it zoomed off into the night. It sped north—toward Connecticut.

Twenty-one

Up moonlit parkways he raced after her, and in the light of his headlights she was standing before him again, a beautiful slender blonde in a long black coat, beckoning, waving to him to stop.

His tires hummed over cement, and she was seated behind him talking—about a man named Wolfgang Corvo, her face pensive, wreathed in clouds of cigarette smoke, her voice delicate as a falling star.

Before his grim bloodshot eyes she raised her dewy face under a white umbrella—and pleaded with him from the back of a cab on a cold blustery night, with a black chiffon scarf whipping its ends across her cheeks.

She stood before him, haggard and buffeted, on the sands of Coney Island. She scurried from him down a pine-shadowed driveway, and zigzagged from him through the crowds, the neon lights of Broadway.

For her he had always been waiting—and from him she had always been running.

He had sacrificed his life for her—his job, his health, his home, his honor. He had lied for her, broken the law for her and trusted her to the point of insanity. And all she had given him in return was fakery, illusion, cruel tricks, betrayal.

Why?

Why had she hated him so?

And why had she found it so necessary that David Marks be destroyed?

Who was she?

As he sped up the turnpikes after the powerful little red car Dave had glimmerings, lightning flashes, but still he did not know.

"Dave . . . Dave."

Jim's voice faded, died away. Jim was out of range. The intercom was silent. The lights of New York City had long since given way to the rolling foothills of Connecticut, and still he could not catch her, overtake her, although sometimes he came close enough to see her shadowy head through the isinglass of her rear window.

She was alone, driving on the right. The car was foreign, English, exactly like the black MG Philip Ferguson had driven.

It was identical to the red MG that the girl Muffin had driven off in on the rainy night of Trench's party. It had Connecticut license plates. So Diana was from Connecticut. Possibly Diana was "Muffin." Dave recalled the words of Mr. Kahn . . . "Perhaps the scene was staged—for a purpose."

What the purpose had been Dave could not decide. Perhaps it had been merely an example of her whimsical cruelty, her love of theatrical effects. What was far more important was that she had to be from Connecticut. She had never lived in New York. She had merely commuted to the city. There had not been one round trip a night on those memorable evenings. There had been two round trips a night. She had probably driven down from Connecticut to the Village and driven back again after Dave had dropped her off. On the night of the murder she had merely melted unseen into her own home territory.

She had of course lied to him about not knowing Ferguson.

She had had to have known him well, well enough to know about his fishing trip, his empty house, his ship-to-shore telephone, and well enough to know about the accident, the car in the quarry. She had been the "anonymous tipster." She had juggled the entire complicated plot in her frail white hands, her icy little hands.

She had shot Ferguson to death in his library. He had come without hesitation at her call. He had been eagerly awaiting her—freshly showered, sipping a drink, with a fire built and the television going—when she walked in and fired a bullet into his back.

138

Who was she?

The landscape flew by. Cemeterial trees lined the road. The tiny red English sports car turned off at the familiar exit.

With the full moon racing him, he pursued the dim red taillights through the familiar winding roads—past woods and quiet settlements, past water glimmering silvery amidst dark hills. His cab rattled and shuddered now, its engine was smoking, and he held his breath, fearful that at any moment it would cough its last. He would be left in these cool still woods with those taillights vanishing like summer fireflies.

Halfway up the last ridge, half a mile from the white gateposts of Ferguson's house, the cab at last gave out. It shuddered to a halt, and he could not get it started again. He climbed out, but when he got to the top of the ridge and looked down into the hollow where Ferguson's property was, he saw the red car parked outside the gateposts with its lights out.

No one was in it. A black chiffon scarf lay on the seat. He picked it up. It smelled of lavender.

Everything was silent. The road leading up to the unlit church steeple was deserted, a silver ribbon in the moonlight. Halfway up the hill Trench's house was pitch-dark, the silhouette of its silo outlined against the luminous sky. It was so still he could hear the sound of bullfrogs croaking from the Ferguson pond deep inside the property. He could see no lights, not even a glow in the sky beyond the pine trees where the house was hidden.

He moved up the driveway.

Underneath the canopy of pungent branches, over the soft bed of pine needles he moved warily, listening. Once he called her name. But there was no answer, and then more swiftly he strode on, reaching the open clearing, the lawn, the shining pond—and the beautiful spectacular house.

Its façade was dark. Its stately reflection shimmered in the moonlit water where the croaking of the bullfrogs seemed to emphasize the idyllic peace of this Eden of wealth and luxury.

Dave called again.

"Diana."

And his voice died. It faded away.

He climbed the shallow brick steps.

The polished anchor gleamed in the moonlight. He let it fall and listened to the echo.

He knocked again, then called, "Mrs. Ferguson?"

There was no answer. But upstairs at one of the dark windows he thought he saw a shadowy face.

"I'm David Marks," he addressed the window. "And I'm looking for a girl who calls herself Diana Roberts. Is she in there with you, Mrs. Ferguson?"

No reply. The face withdrew from the window. A white curtain fluttered and was still.

Dave raised his voice slightly. "I'm sure she is," he said. "I chased her all the way up here. And her car's outside. It's a red MG." Still there was no answer, no movement from inside the house. Trying to keep his voice even, he said, "She's blond, about twenty-five years old. She wears boots and a long black coat." He waved the black chiffon scarf aloft. "She was wearing this tonight."

Every window remained dark. The tree shadows flickered. The bullfrogs croaked.

"Please, Mrs. Ferguson. Please help me. I'm the guy who's been accused of killing your husband," he said. "The cabdriver. But I didn't kill him. *She* did."

No response.

The walls breathed silence.

It was as though he were addressing an empty house—or a tomb.

"She knew your husband," he said. "She knew about that car. She knew all about that accident. It was she who called the police."

From somewhere he thought he heard a cry. And for an instant he thought the face appeared again at the window.

"Why won't you help me, Mrs. Ferguson?" Dave called to her. His voice was choked. "Why won't you *answer* me?"

When again the response was only cold forbidding silence, he tried the door. He knocked again. He banged on it. Then he put his shoulder to it. It did not give. He kicked it. He heard a chain rattle from inside, but nothing else.

"Okay," he muttered. He ran down the steps. Circling the house, crouched over like an animal, he tried windows, doors, frantically clawing at them, battering at them, and tugging and wrenching at the top section of the Dutch door which once had been so temptingly open.

"*Diana!*" he yelled. "Open up. I know you're in there!"

At any moment he expected to hear sirens—see a police car.

Finally he stooped down and wrested a brick loose from the terrace. He smashed a glass pane in the top of the Dutch door. The glass fell to the bricks with a crash and a tinkle. Pain creased across his wrist and blood gushed warm over his fingers as he reached inside and turned the key.

"*Diana! Mrs. Ferguson!*"

His voice echoed. He could hear the sound of his own harsh breath panting in the moonlit silence. He was in a hallway lit by moonlight. A clock was ticking. It began to chime—mellow tones falling measuredly on the air, and when it was done, from far, far off, he heard a faint "ping," a delicate chime in echo.

"Mrs. Ferguson."

He began to grope along the wall, feeling for light switches, straining his eyes into doorways and up staircases. The dim shapes of furniture loomed. Crystal chandeliers glittered. Mirrors shimmered with strange illusions. He smelled the spicy odor of pink carnations in a vase that toppled as he went by, and the sickening sweet scent of lavender. At any moment around a corner he expected to encounter her—in her long pale lilac robe.

"Answer me," he whispered hoarsely to the shadows. "Why are you afraid to answer me?"

He thought he heard the rustle of draperies across a rug. He thought he heard an in-drawn breath, a gasp of fear. For a moment in a huge mirror facing him he thought he saw a shadowy reflection, a pale face with enormous eyes. Then it disappeared around a corner.

"Diana! *You're* Diana!"

But she was gone.

Her back to him, with long dark hair flying, she fled down a long dim tunnel of hallway.

"Wait, Mrs. Ferguson!"

And it was all finally coming clear.

He had been deceived by the hair, the dark hair—but even Momma had spoken of a wig. In the wind, in the bright light of day, she had always worn a scarf or a turban. He had been deceived by Portugal—but Portugal was a country in turmoil.

She had never gone abroad. She had simply hidden somewhere—maybe even in this house.

And on a dark night she had called her husband in Florida, told him she had something to tell him.

141

That something was undoubtedly the accident.

And whether her motive for killing him had been horror and shame or merely the desire to get rid of him and inherit his fortune, she had walked into the library that night and shot him in cold blood. Then she had hidden while Dave came in to look for her, and after he left, she had fled.

She had high cheekbones, she was part Russian. She had been in TV, and she came from the Middle West, Dr. Corvo's Middle West, from Cicero, Illinois.

Like a bubble expanding, it came clearer and clearer, and he heard himself shouting it to her, shouting wild accusations as he lurched down the hallway after her, and dived in just behind her as she darted into a pitch-dark room.

"You're Diana, Mrs. Ferguson!"

It was exultation even to know that at least she was real—not a dybbuk, not a phantom.

"You'll never get away with it!"

His voice rang through the darkness. He grabbed for a floating drapery. He heard a piece of furniture crash—and then a cry. His hand encountered soft cold flesh . . . an arm. She screamed.

"Leave me alone."

He stood rooted for a second, his grip relaxing, and she broke loose. With a rush she went past him, something clattered, and a light went on—and she was wheeling round to him in the light of a lamp, pointing a pistol at his chest.

"Get out!" She glared at him. "You're insane!"

Dave stood staring at her.

"Oh, my God," he whispered. "Oh, my God."

She wasn't Diana Roberts.

She stood facing him in the book-lined room where her husband's body had lain, and she had masses of coal-black hair, coarse and curly, dark eyes and a round pink face. She looked like a frightened milkmaid.

"Get out, or I'll shoot," she said.

"I'm sorry."

"Don't come any nearer."

She brandished the gun clumsily. Even her voice wasn't Diana's voice. It was flat, nasal and unmodulated.

"Mrs. Ferguson, I apologize. I've made a terrible mistake."

"Never mind. Just get out."

She advanced from behind the desk, still brandishing the gun, but he stood his ground in the center of the dark red rug where a month ago Philip Ferguson's body had lain. "Mrs. Ferguson, please, may I ask you a question before I go. There's a red MG outside your gates. Does it belong to you?" he asked.

"No," she said.

"Do you know who it does belong to?"

She stared at him haughtily, raising her chin and then one black tweezed eyebrow. She would be fat in a couple of years.

"I don't see that it's necessary to tell you."

"Oh, my God!" he said bitterly. "I chased that car all the way from New York. It belongs to that girl I've been looking for now—for almost a month. She lives somewhere around here. She has to. I know she does. She knew your husband, and I'm sure she shot him. And if I don't find her, Mrs. Ferguson, I'm finished. I'm done for!"

His voice reverberated through the dark mazes of the house.

"You don't have to *shout,* for heaven's sake!"

Tossing her head, she crossed to a window and raised it. She fanned her face with her hand. Then, still holding the gun in the other hand, she faced him, her dark, round, rather bovine eyes roving over his shaggy hair, his haggard face, his filthy clothes. She laid the gun down on the desk.

"The car belongs to a friend of mine," she said in a stiff voice.

"Thank you," Dave said. "Who?"

"But her name is not Diana."

"Of course it isn't. Who?"

She walked up and down, twisting her rings. On every finger was an enormous diamond. "And I can't possibly believe that she'd do anything that you've described. She's quite nice, utterly respectable, quite decent, and we've always been more than kind to her—and her poor alcoholic brother. She couldn't have killed my husband. She didn't *know* him well enough."

"I see." Dave was backing off. He was beginning to see the truth.

"And my husband totally ignored her." She twisted a diamond, staring reflectively at the moonlight. "I'm sure you're much mistaken, Mr. Marks."

"Okay," he said. "But could you just please tell me her name?"

"Of course. Why not?" She smiled her slightly superior smile. "Since I'm sure the poor thing's innocent. It's—"

But even as she was saying the name he expected to hear, a shot rang out. She swayed and screamed, then crumpled at his feet—in a heap of lavender chiffon.

Twenty-two

"Good God!"

He knelt beside her. As he lifted the soft limp wrist, another shot rang out. It hit the mantelpiece above his head.

"For God's sake!"

Through the library window he heard footsteps running and glimpsed a slender shadow darting toward the pond.

"Diana!"

He raced out the library doorway and back through the maze of rooms. In a cavernous hall the front door stood open on a wide vista of moonlight.

Another shot crackled.

He leaped back with a yell.

Amidst floating gunsmoke he spied her running—in the high black boots with the long black coat hanging from her shoulders and long brown hair hanging lank. "Diana, stop! What the hell do you think you're doing?"

She did not stop. She kept running around the pond. In a ray of moonlight he glimpsed her face, pale, fixed, a silver mask. Her hair clung to her head like the hair of someone drowned.

"Come on. You can't go around killing people forever. For God's sake, I know who you are."

Across the sheet of shining water she raised the gun. She fired.

This time the bullet grazed his cheek.

Stung with pain, he flung himself down the steps of the house, threw himself into the water, and then as she continued to fire insanely, as the bullets spattered across the water's surface, he dived, dived deep into the freezing murky depths. He swam, holding his breath, as Robert Trench had once held his—in the golden days, the Happy Era, the glorious reign of Philip Ferguson.

When he surfaced, she was standing with her back to him a couple of feet away, with the rifle at the ready, pointing it out over the water. He could see the rifle shaking. She looked like a child, a skinny frightened kid with bony cheekbones in a long black rag-bag coat. Her teeth were chattering.

In another second he had grabbed her ankle. He twisted it and she tottered to the ground. When she was on her back, screaming and struggling to rise, he grabbed her right wrist, wrenched the rifle from her grasp and hurled it into the water.

"Dumbbell. Idiot."

"Let me go. Get your hands off me."

She who had been so sweet, so gentle, was struggling, screaming, clawing, panting, kicking—even biting him.

As he held her arms down and straddled her thin young flailing body with his soaking wet and muddy legs, she fought to rise, then batted her head up and down on the grass and turned and twisted her neck like an animal being branded. Finally, utterly spent, she lay still, breathing heavily. Then she began to weep. Big tears rolled down from her closed eyes, with their skimpy eyelashes, down the gaunt hollows of her cheeks. Sobs convulsed her body.

"Margaret," he said quietly. "Your name is Margaret."

She did not answer. The tears flowed.

"Margaret Carson. You're Trench's secretary."

She shook her head.

"Look," Dave said, still straddling her, half kneeling on the chilly ground. "I *know* you're Margaret Carson. I even know something about your life. You wrote a book called *Moose* with Robert Trench, and you own a red MG. Your brother calls you Muffin. He drinks. His name is Joe."

She opened her eyes briefly, stared at him, then closed them again.

"You've done very well at keeping yourself hidden," he said. "But the question is *why*, Miss Carson? Why did you have to do it?"

"Don't mock me," she said in low, tearful tones. She turned her face from him, burying it in the grass.

"I'm not mocking you. Why, in the first place, did you murder Philip Ferguson?" he asked. "Because he was evil—a slob and a hit-and-run driver? On moral principles? Or just because you were jealous—of Mrs. Ferguson?"

"Ugh," she said.

"Did they do something to offend you? Hurt you?"

"No," she said, with her face still pressed to the ground. "Why do *you* care?"

"Because I do. Because murder is horrible. Because I don't really know you, and can't possibly understand." When she did not answer, he asked, "You couldn't have been in love with that monster?"

"No, God, no" came the choked reply.

"He didn't rape you or get you pregnant?"

"No."

"Then what?"

"I'm not going to tell you," she said in a stifled voice with her face still turned away. "So just kill me and get it over with."

"I'm not going to kill you."

She lay there like a stone.

The water from his body dripped slowly on her neck.

Dave addressed the back of her head, the thin hair straggling over the white scalp, straggling over the black coat collar.

"What did I ever do to you?" he burst out suddenly. "What kind of crazy gimmick was that, and how did you think you could ever get away with it? Eighty dollars to Stamford! A matter of life and death! It was loathsome. It was diabolical." His voice rose. "I can't imagine any sane person pulling a trick like that on another human being."

"So, kill me," she said.

"Come on, Margaret. Why did you do it? What the hell possessed you?" He shook her shoulder. "Come on. Answer me." He wrenched her head around, held her chin so that her pale, set face with its closed eyes faced him like a dead face, with the moon painting it the color of lead. He shook her. "Why me? *Me?*" He shook her again. "*Why? Why?* You little bitch!"

Her lips moved at last.

"It was—fantasy."

"Fantasy?"

She kept her eyes shut. "Diana Roberts," she murmured. Then she opened them. She looked at him with just an echo of her old beautiful pensive look, and her voice held just an echo of its old thrilling sweetness. "She was fantasy. Pure fantasy. The best I ever dreamed." She gazed at him sadly, emptily. "I loved her. Wasn't she beautiful? Romantic?"

"A liar. A cheat," Dave growled.

"But you loved her."

With a ghastly wistfulness she was looking up into his eyes. And for a moment he felt pity. For a moment he could see her trapped up there in that house day after day. He could hear the click of typewriter keys and see the dreary pages piling up. He could see her peering down over that low stone wall from the flagstone patio at twilight, listening to the cocktail conversation below, the clink of glasses and the twang of tennis balls. He remembered the lavender lipstick and the chiffon scarf drenched with perfume.

But pity was dangerous, more dangerous than gunfire.

"Come on," he said. He rose from the grass, jerking her upward, tugging at her arm. "We're driving in to Stamford."

"No!"

She tried to throw herself back on the ground.

"I'm not going. You can't make me. If you do, I'll lie." Once again a skinny little virago, she doubled up in his grasp. "I'll just tell them you're crazy—I never saw you in my life!"

"Come on."

"I'll even tell them you shot Sharon."

"Shut up."

He picked her up. He began carrying her toward the driveway. She kicked and struggled. "Please, David, please." She writhed and beat her fists against his chest. "Don't make me go. Don't make me talk. If you do, I'll kill myself."

"I've heard all that before."

She began to cry, in huge convulsive sobs. He kept on walking toward the pine trees.

"If you stop a minute, if you let me down, I'll tell you why I had to murder him."

"*Had* to?"

"Yes," she sobbed.

He set her down. He still held tight to her. "All right—so why did you?"

She stood rigidly for a moment. Then she raised her head to the moon, the stars. "Because—he threatened me," she began. Then she broke off. "For the simple reason—I didn't trust him." Again she broke off, and then in low, intense, rapid-fire tones, she said, "David, why don't you just leave well enough alone? I—I made a terrible mistake in ever doing what I did to you. I—panicked. I was crazy. I didn't know you, know what you were like, I thought I was made of steel and you weren't human or intelligent, I lived in a world of fantasy, of crazy values with that awful man and those awful people, I should have just kept teaching speech in that little Indian school." All the sentences were run together like water rushing down a gorge.

"That still doesn't help me," he said, "The police are going to arrest me. They're going to send me to prison."

"I know, but it's much better to go to prison."

"*Prison!* I have two kids!"

"Yes," she interrupted quickly. "David, don't make me tell. Don't make me—*please!*" She tried to tear her hand loose from his grasp.

"Why did he threaten you?"

"*Please!*" she whispered brokenly. She stood there staring at the ground.

He kept looking at her agonized face, her blinking eyes, her drooping head with its limp hair, and finally he asked the question. "Did it have something to do with the car, the accident—my wife?"

For a long moment she paused. "Yes," she answered in a strangled voice.

"What?"

She raised her head.

"What?" he repeated.

She was hovering on the brink now, with eyes so huge, so glassy that slowly, finally, like a black crevice opening in the earth, the truth began to yawn across his soul.

"*What?*"

Her hand felt cold. It felt like stone—like marble in his grasp.

"I didn't mean to," she faltered. "It was just one date, one

149

evening, one crazy invitation on his part. He took me—driving. And drinking. Then we stopped off at the Waldorf . . . and went to bed together. A—a fantasy."

"October sixteenth? *You* were with him?"

She nodded numbly. He gripped her cold hand hard.

"What didn't you mean . . . to do?" he choked.

"He—got sick. His foot hurt. And I didn't see her . . . I swear."

He let her cold hand fall. "But *he* was driving. I *saw* him."

"The—the wheel was on the right, David."

Her voice died.

The world fell silent.

The stars turned upside down, and he was seeing a face turning and swiveling at him, a face with a black eye patch, staring back at him long after the car had sped on.

For a long moment they stood there, like two statues facing each other, a man and a woman carved out of black marble, and then he sank slowly to his knees, and she began to run, scrambling from him though he did not stir from his kneeling position, and running from him up the steep incline, over the rocky ledges and the tangled underbrush dividing Trench's property from Philip Ferguson's, running as she had run perhaps on the night of Ferguson's murder, climbing as she had climbed that night toward the one refuge she knew.

On the grass below, Dave's head came to rest against the earth. He did not see her or pay the slightest attention to her until she had reached the top, the border of bright stars, and stood for a moment looking down at him, then up at the moon, cold and white and implacable in the sky.

"Diana!"

He started to his feet. But it was too late.

With a cry she leaped, her slight body flying above him in the long loose coat, the shining, twisting boots, down into the silvery waters of the pond.

He dived and dived for her. Numbly he groped in the black cold murky water, parting weeds and clawing through ooze deep down. But she was nowhere to be found.

Finally he climbed out and went into the house, walking wearily once more through the labyrinthine rooms of Philip Ferguson's dark and silent domain. In the library Mrs. Ferguson was moaning softly. He knelt beside her in his dripping filthy rags and pressed her hand. Then he moved to the telephone. He dialed.

"Give me the police," he said.

About the Author

LUCILLE FLETCHER is best known for her suspense classic *Sorry, Wrong Number*, originally a radio play, later a novel, TV play and motion picture. She has written extensively for both screen and television, and is the author of several successful mystery novels, including *Blindfold, . . . And Presumed Dead, The Strange Blue Yawl* and *The Girl in Cabin B54*. She is the author of the recently successful Broadway play, *Night Watch*, which was also a motion picture starring Elizabeth Taylor. A native of Brooklyn, Lucille Fletcher now lives on the eastern shore of Maryland with her husband, novelist Douglass Wallop.